An Historical
Irish Mail Order Bride
Romance

Una's Crossroads

Una's Crossroads

Katherine St. Clair

Copyright and Disclaimer

All right reserved. © 2015 Katherine St. Clair and Maplewood Publishing. No part of this publication may be copied, reproduced in any format, by any means, electronic or otherwise, without the permission or consent from the copyright owner and publisher of this book.

This book is a work of fiction. The names, characters, places, events, and incidents are products' of the author's imagination or have been used fictitiously and are not to be construed as real. Any resemblance to persons, living or dead, actual events, locales or organizations is entirely coincidental.

ISBN-13: 978-1523478453
ISBN-10:1523478454

Printed in the United States

Contents

Contents _____ 5
Chapter One _____ 1
Chapter Two _____ 11
Chapter Three _____ 21
Chapter Four _____ 31
Chapter Five _____ 41
Chapter Six _____ 51
Chapter Seven _____ 59
Chapter Eight _____ 71
Chapter Nine _____ 79
Chapter Ten _____ 97
Chapter Eleven _____ 103
Chapter Twelve _____ 107
Chapter Thirteen _____ 115
Chapter Fourteen _____ 125
Chapter Fifteen _____ 141
Chapter Sixteen _____ 153
Chapter Seventeen _____ 161
Chapter Eighteen _____ 173
Chapter Nineteen _____ 181
Chapter Twenty _____ 187
Chapter Twenty-One _____ 201
A Note to my Readers _____ 211
An Excerpt from Under a Texas Sky _____ 213
More books from Katherine St.Clair _____ 216

Chapter One

Una and McKenna Brady had been awake for hours. They sat aboveboard on the ship "Betty Gregg" under the dark night sky waiting for morning. They were pressed together for warmth.

When they had been sleeping below deck on their bunks, Una had awakened in the middle of the night to a smell she'd come to recognize in the past six months. The smell of decomposing flesh. The woman who had been sleeping next to her was dead. Una and her sister McKenna came up to the deck. Even though it was cold, it was better than down there with everybody.

So many people had already died onboard that Una and McKenna could see sharks following the ship because of all the bodies that had been thrown overboard.

Una knew that McKenna was hungry. Una was hungry too. They'd had to bring their own supply of food that had been nearly impossible for the girls since they didn't have any food to begin with. They'd had to save up part of their daily pound of "stirabout," a mix of Indian corn and rice mixed in water and a four-ounce slice of bread. During their two months in County Cork waiting for the very voyage they were now on, they'd had to wait in line all day for the small amount of nutrition that had kept them alive.

The ship had entitled each girl to an allotment of two pints of water every day. Now the ship was running dry. Everyone on board had been rationed down from the already insufficient amount. When the ship had set sail from Cork harbor, there had been a pervading sense of hope. This had lasted for a precious short period of time. Soon, the fear that had hung over every Irishman on their home soil had crept on board.

Una and McKenna shared a bunk with two strangers they'd never met before. During harsh storms, vomit and sometimes worse would drip from the bunk above them.

It had only taken a few days and the first few deaths for fear to settle over each passenger on the ship.

The Ireland that Una had grown up in was barren. The potato blight had continued past all speculation and didn't seem to be ending. People were dying every day of starvation and illness, including cholera. Yet there was still a strength in Ireland's people that rose up time and again.

A tight hand grasped Una's arm. Una looked down to see that her sixteen-year-old-sister had fallen asleep. Sleep for both girls was riddled with nightmares. Visions of their parents, four brothers, and their two older sisters falling victim to disease swam through their heads day and night. Una knew that McKenna was seeing it all over again now. Everyone but the two girls and one of their brothers had been taken within four days.

Four days that were now burned into both girls' minds.

Una had been waiting for it to come to her. The violent stomach pains that made their mother cry out, bloody waste, vomiting, and fever.

Their father had been delirious before his death, screaming at his own demons.

Their brother Kieran was a year older than Una, and when their father died, he became the natural leader. The three of them had sold the remaining farm animals and everything from the house. There was no money to pay rent, and no strength for the three remaining children to try and plant again.

They'd headed on foot across country roads from Molls Gap to Queenstown, County Cork. As they walked past the little homes, they had found more death. Whole families taken by disease. People who looked dead but were still alive. There were people who had died along the road and lay untouched, decaying where they had fallen.

The three Brady siblings were already so wasted from malnutrition that the walking was very hard. They could walk for barely four hours a day, and this was only when done slowly. On the fourth day, the girls woke up to what sounded like a wild animal. It was their brother.

Kieran's groans of pain were deep, guttural, horrifying. His stomach cramped, and he evacuated more water than he'd had to drink in days. Una had walked over ravaged fields to find water and bring it back to Kieran, but when she got back, he was gone. Just like their parents, he'd died quickly in the midst of great pain.

The girl's split the water between them. They were too exhausted to cry, too weak to mourn for their brother. They could only look forward.

"McKenna," Una whispered into her sister's ear. She brushed her hand down her younger sister's face hoping she might think the touch came from their mother. She brushed McKenna's hair back and kissed her forehead. "McKenna," she said again as McKenna flinched in her sleep.

The girl's blue eyes opened wildly, her jaw and body shaking with the fear of what she'd been seeing. Unfortunately, it wouldn't be much different from nightmare to reality.

"You were having a nightmare," Una explained to the fearful look in McKenna's eyes. "Everything will be okay now. We'll be in Boston in a few days, and everything will be just fine."

"I want to go home." McKenna said softly.

Una exhaled. "I know. Me too." But both girls knew that home no longer existed. There was no family to go back to, no farmland, and no house. Kieran had been right. They needed to leave while they had the small amount of money they'd made off of their animals and possessions. It had been his idea to go to County Cork. His idea to find a ship to take them across the Atlantic. They would get on a ship bound for Canada or America. They just needed to get away.

Una had thought naively that they just needed to make it long enough to get on the ship. That once they were on the ship, everything would be okay. But now she'd watched more people die. She'd lost track of the days they'd been on the sea for weeks, but how many? Una was half the size of her former self. McKenna too. They were no more than bones with a covering of skin.

"Do you think we'll be there soon?" McKenna asked. She looked like she hadn't grown much since the blight started three years ago. She was small for her age, still the size of a thirteen-year-old. Their mother had been the opposite. Within the span of two and a half years, their mother had aged tremendously. The once beautiful Irish woman with wide, childbearing hips seemed like a crinkled-up old woman just before she died.

"Yes, soon." Una looked up to the sky. "Look, can you find Draco?" She looked up to the stars looking for the constellation.

"There," McKenna said pointing to the sky.

"So it is," Una smiled. During the nights of the past two and a half months, they'd slept outside, under the stars. They'd stared into the sky looking for signs of their existence and found the constellations that their father used to show them shining back at them. Now, since they'd come aboard, the same sky full of stars had brought them comfort.

"What about Orion?" Una asked.

"Too easy," some long-lost, youthful sound came back to McKenna's voice. The younger girl turned her head up with a knowing look on her face. "There." She flicked her finger to the sky, and Una hugged her sister close to her.

"Well, then that…" Una pointed further to the west, "…must be the 'great top hat.' You must have heard of that one."

"No such thing," McKenna said.

"How do you know? That certainly looks like a top hat to me."

"And that," McKenna pointed south of Una's top hat, "looks like the 'great wood mouse.'"

"Well, I do believe you may be right."

Una looked around at her countrymen. A mother rocking a baby, and men, who may have had a feud at home, were bound together here. She watched another girl their age, sitting alone, looking to the sky.

"Trasna na dtonnta, dul siar, dul siar," Una's voice quavered out alone into the dark. The song was one they all knew. Children were taught the words in primary school, a song about going over the waves, a song about going home. "Slán leis an uaigneas 'is slán leis an gcian…" Una's voice was met by McKenna's soft voice. One of the men across the way gave his baritone to the task, and it rang out proud and strong, "My heart rises in me with the break of each day, as I draw closer to the land of my people!"

The man next to him sang, and the mother with her child sang, until the knot of Irish men and women created a sound that rang out into the night. "Geal é mo chroí, agus geal í an ghrian." It was a sound Una had not heard for a long time, the sound of brotherhood, of strength, the sound of something new coming bright over the horizon. "Geal a bheith ag filleadh go hÉirinn!"

When the sounds of the voices dimmed, the light they had created remained, and Una sat under it like she was being swaddled in a vast warm blanket.

Una snuggled into her sister, gazing up at the sky, until she fell asleep. She awoke with a start as the sun was coming up and a loud sound came from somewhere on the ship. When Una opened her eyes, she realized it wasn't one sound but more of a collective group of sounds. McKenna was standing in the spot where she'd been sitting only a few minutes ago. Una stood up to join her.

Una looked at her sister and then at the horizon where McKenna was looking.

America.

After so many days that Una had lost count, so many people dying off, water scarce, food non-existent, after leaving a ravaged Ireland where everyone seemed to have turned to a skeleton if they weren't already dead… after all that, they were here. Boston.

"We've made it," Una's heart was beating quickly.

McKenna reached down and grabbed her sister's hand. "What will it be like?"

"I guess we'll find out," Una smiled.

The ride in to shore was unbearable. Everyone was standing on deck and even with a good eighty of the three hundred passengers now dead, the human cargo pushing toward the railing where Una and McKenna were standing had trapped them in place.

There was no way to get out or push around the other passengers, all craning to see the great escape for which they were headed.

The moment they were close enough to see, more people filled their vision. Lots of people. Ragged, dirty people mixed with a finer sort of person, but many more poor than the other. As the ship got closer, Una realized that all the ragged, dirty people were their people. They were Irishmen. A flutter moved through Una's stomach. She was so hungry that she'd been dreaming about food as much as she'd been dreaming about the death of her family. Were those people eating? They still looked so thin, so poor.

It took hours for the ship to come in to dock, to lower the gangplank and begin letting the passengers come down. The people on the docks stared at them. Some were like their own faces, like looking into a mirror. People waiting for news of their land, of their families. The shipload of new immigrants was a spectacle to others. Una held onto McKenna very tightly, as if someone were about to take her away. McKenna clung to her sister with a strength that surprised Una.

The stench of the people on board was floating up Una's nose. Without the help of the ocean breeze to carry it off, it mixed with the smell of fish and the collective miasma of all the poor people who now stood dockside. Mingling with the ship's ragged bodies, there expelled an intense putrid mélange of foul stink.

Una felt an odd compulsion to stay on the ship, though it had been her daily source of fresh torture for the past weeks.

McKenna pulled at Una's hand, and soon the two were walking toward the gangplank with one grubby little bundle the only thing to carry along.

"More filthy Irish," a yell came from an unseen face in the crowd of people on the dock. The girls saw the man who had just yelled as he was pushed and expelled from the crowd. Her own people were here just as they were there. A small smile touched her lips.

Some people on the dock were moving, some working, and others were just staring at each person as they moved off the ship. A fine-looking woman stopped her walking and looked at the decamping passengers. The woman caught Una's eyes. Una held her gaze. She was not an Irish woman, but her stare was not mean. Was it compassion? It felt to Una that perhaps it was simply one woman seeing another. One woman, who though life had separated them, was not so very different from the other. The woman walked on with two well-dressed gentlemen at her side. Una's stomach curdled with envy.

If only Una and McKenna were on their way to a warm home, with a hot dinner, milk, water, and fresh clothes. If only there were a safe, soft bed waiting for them. Una pushed her fingernails into the flesh of her hand. It wasn't right to be ungrateful. Though things were bad, she was alive, and she had McKenna. They'd made it this far and would soon be somewhere safe, with hot food, a good bed, and honest work. It was blasphemous to be ungrateful when she had hope ahead of her.

Una took a deep breath. They had a long time yet before they were in Missouri. No matter how much they were disliked or looked down upon, Una and McKenna were going to see their way there.

"Go back to where you came from," an angry voice yelled from Una's left. Una lifted her chin a bit higher and pressed McKenna's hand into hers. A child was crying from somewhere back in the ship. McKenna paused, and Una looked back. McKenna's hands were shaking.

Una said, "We're fine. We have a place to be. Everything's okay now."

McKenna nodded and began moving again. As soon as they were off the ship, Una moved them into the winding buildings and roads that created the city.

After Kieran died and the girls had made it to County Cork, Una and McKenna had stayed in the city while they made their plan. Una had bought boat fare for herself and McKenna two months hence, but it took all the money they had. Una had written to their mother's sister, Catherine Donnelly, who lived in America. She'd written to see if her aunt could arrange a life for them in America.

Their aunt had written back that she'd been able to make a match for both girls. She lived in farming country, and though the girls would bring nothing with them to the marriages, the men would appreciate hard-working women who knew how to farm the land. Una had written back with thanks and the request of financial assistance from Boston to Missouri, something Una would pay back as soon as she had any money. This letter had left without time for a reply, and Una wasn't sure if there would be help awaiting them in Boston, or if they would have to make their way to Missouri on their own. Her aunt had mentioned a man who ran a covered wagon out her way. In Una's letter, she'd asked for her aunt to leave word with the man Catherine had mentioned. If there was any assistance to be had, it would be there.

Chapter Two

"Where are we going?" McKenna asked as they walked hand-in-hand through the crowded streets of Boston.

"Aunt Catherine said we're to go to the Mill Dam and ask around for the Hill brothers."

"Where is the Mill Dam?" McKenna followed quickly behind Una.

Una looked around, "I don't know. I suppose we'll have to find someone to ask." Each person that Una looked at seemed busy and not to be bothered with two girls in such a state of obvious poverty as Una and McKenna were.

Already Una's legs were beginning to hurt. Her breath was heavy in her lungs from the exercise, and she wasn't sure how far she could walk. They'd barely eaten anything on the ship, and they hadn't had any real use of their legs while on board. Now, Una felt weak and unsure of her footsteps.

Una could feel her younger sister's eyes on her. She knew they couldn't continue walking like this either. Though they were only a few hundred feet from the ship they'd just disembarked, Una was exhausted. Any extra unnecessary movement was painful to think about, let alone accomplish.

"Ok. We'll ask someone," Una looked around herself. She opened her mouth to ask a man rushing by, but he moved with such force and in a way that excluded the world around him that Una shrank back.

"Maybe in a store?" McKenna suggested as the two of them stood, unmoving in the middle of the street. Una nodded absently.

People, horses, carts, and carriages were moving at a speed that pushed them closer and closer to the sides of the road. Soon Una pushed McKenna, forcing them both out of the way of a fast-approaching wagon that threated to run them over if they didn't move quickly enough. Both girls watched the wagon pass with wide eyes as they barely made it in time.

They walked to the nearest storefront. A cobbler. The windows were impenetrable by the human eye. Una squinted, then walked to the door and let herself in. The shop consisted of one tiny room the size of a four-person carriage. There was a man working on a piece of leather, and he did not look up.

"Excuse me," Una said with hesitation. The man said nothing. Una looked at McKenna who seemed confused as well. "Excuse me," she repeated.

"Can't ya read?" The man said without looking up.

"I'm sorry?" Una looked around her, seeing nothing to read.

"The sign, clear as day."

Una looked around herself again, then saw a small rectangle in the window. She looked to the man who did not appear willing to say more so she took McKenna by the hand and walked her sister out of the shop. Once outside, she turned and looked at the sign that sat mostly obscured by the thick glass.

"*No Irish need apply*," the sign said. Una's stomach hardened.

"Come on," Una took McKenna's hand again pushed back into the shop. "I wasn't looking for a job, and if I were, I would never want to work for the likes of a man like you." She whirled around before the man could respond.

They walked quickly past the shop, Una's head held high, her stomach clenching. She walked past the next few shops just to regain her composure from the surprise of such a sign and the surprise of such rudeness.

Her countrymen were hospitable. Even as they were poor and starving, they were friendly and welcoming. These people, well, this man…

Una slowed down and looked to the next few signs to see what might be their best choice. They weren't even asking for anything. They weren't beggars, not looking for handouts, they only wanted information about a location.

She scoured the windows looking for similar signs as the other one or other signs that said they would not be welcome inside.

Gathering her strength, Una entered a curved brown door. She was unsure what exactly the shop was for, but it seemed to have something to do with maritime business. This time Una stepped boldly into the shop and began to speak almost as soon as the door shut behind her and McKenna. She did not want to be mistaken for anything but what she was.

"I'm looking for the Mill Dam. Could you please tell me where I'm to go?" She directed the question generally to the room at large, then focused on the three people who stood in the space.

There were two women and a man, all of whom looked up at Una's words. McKenna squeezed Una's hand tightly making her spine even stiffer.

"You're a ways away yet," the oldest woman spoke in a soft, familiar voice. Immediately Una sighed out a breath. The woman was Irish.

"If you could just tell us the direction to go, we'll be on our way."

The woman looked at both girls.

"You're just off the boat, eh?" The woman looked to the man who must have been her husband. The man made a little move with his head that Una couldn't comprehend.

Una nodded her head apprehensively. Perhaps being just off the boat was a bad thing. Another person to contend with? Or maybe they thought that their bony bodies and physical disarray would make all the Irish look bad? Or perhaps thought they may carry disease— which, under the circumstances, wasn't such a strange thing to think.

"Why don't you come with me?" the woman said. "You'll have something to eat and drink before you go."

Una's heart filled. It was not what she was expecting. Not kindness. Not after everything.

Una opened her mouth to speak, but her emotions overcame her, and she just nodded instead.

The woman moved and took Una by the hand. She led her through the back of the shop into a small room. It was bare and smaller than the store itself, but Una could tell that the three people, perhaps more, all lived in this tiny space. There was a very small table in the corner.

"Sit here," the woman said. She put part of a loaf of bread, a small bit of cheese, and water together on the table in front of the girls. The woman sat down with them and motioned to the food. Neither Una nor McKenna moved. "It's for you," The woman said gesturing once again to the food and water in front of them.

Una tentatively reached for the bread and broke off a piece, handing it to McKenna. McKenna held the bread, then looked to her sister once again for approval before eating, which she did hungrily. Una smiled, then drank down a full glass of water. It was delicious. The best thing she'd ever put in her mouth. Everything on the ship had grown stale. Somehow even the water had seemed stale.

The woman tried to look away as they ate, but she was unable to. Una found her watching the two of them with interest.

"Thank you," Una said to the woman with food in her mouth.

The woman smiled and nodded. "Where are you two from?"

"Molls Gap," McKenna said. To Una, McKenna sounded in better spirits than she had in a long time.

"We came from Mayo, up north. Still have family there," the woman said in a way that let Una know she was worried for her family. *And she should be,* Una thought.

"I'm Una, this is my youngest sis—" Una paused, "this is my sister, McKenna." McKenna would no longer be her youngest sister, she would be her only sister. The thought startled Una for a moment.

"It's nice to meet you." The woman smiled but did not introduce herself, which Una found odd. But people were odd since the famine and the disease. It was something she'd come to realize and accept. If the woman had introduced herself or her family, then Una would have asked about the woman's travels to America, but the woman's silence kept her from asking.

When both McKenna and Una had had something to eat and drink, their stomachs pulsing from the irregular presence of food, the woman gave them directions to the Mill Dam and to a boarding house near it where they might be able to find cheap boarding.

"Boston is not friendly to us right now. We are too many, starving and poor, and people have become resentful of us." The woman explained to the girls. "There isn't enough room for all of us. We spill into the streets, living like animals, unable to get jobs, and because we live like animals, many treat us like them too."

Una looked at McKenna, whose eyes were turned to her hands.

"Thank you," Una said, "for being so kind to us—"

"You are alone and scared, but you will make it. I can see it in your eyes." The woman looked from Una to McKenna. "You are strong girls. Now, I will point you in the right direction." They walked to the door, and the woman pointed the way down the street for them to go.

Once they were walking, Una and McKenna both moved forward in silence, both intensely feeling the food and drink in their bellies and the words of the woman.

The woman's directions had been clear, and they arrived at the Mill Dam without one wrong turn.

"Excuse me," Una said to a woman selling vegetables on the side of the road. "I'm looking for the Hill brothers. Do you know where I can find them?"

The woman looked at Una and pointed with her head. "One of 'em's right there," she said. Both girls turned to see a man in shabby clothes cleaning something in his hands. There was no sign of a wagon as far as Una could see and nothing to indicate his business.

"That man?" Una pointed making sure she was looking at the right man.

"I said it," The woman said, and Una nodded, afraid to ask anything more. She took her sister's hand once more and walked her over to the man who sat hunched on a barrel.

"Excuse me," Una said to the man. The man did not register that he heard her, if in fact he did. Una stepped closer and spoke louder. "Excuse me, are you one of the Hill brothers?"

The man stopped cleaning the shiny thing in his hand. He'd heard her, but the man didn't look at her, he only looked down to the side where her feet were.

"My aunt, Catherine Donnelly, said you would be able to take us to St. Joseph, Missouri. I think she may have left a note or letter with you?"

The man said nothing to this and refocused his gaze back on the thing he was polishing in his hands. A sinking feeling moved through Una. Without this man and his brother, they had no money and no way of getting to Missouri. The man just kept staring down at what he was cleaning as if he couldn't hear Una.

"Please, my name is Una Brady and this is my sister McKenna Brady—"

"—I've heard about you from your aunt," a new voice came from behind Una. She whirled around to find another man, stout and pock-marked, standing behind them. He was older than the seated man, and he looked Una straight in the eye. "That's my brother, Seamus. He doesn't speak anymore. Got a bad bout of fever as a young one, and he's never been the same since." The man tapped his head with his pointer finger. "But he's a good sort and a hard worker."

"Oh," Una looked back to the seated brother who was staring into his lap.

"I'm Colin Hill." He appraised the girls for a moment before continuing. "You'll have to board here for another two days before we go. There's a family who'll be coming on the journey with us, and we'll have to wait for them."

Una tried to imagine how they would manage to pay their way in Boston for two whole days.

"Will you be able to survive a wagon trip?" he asked. He looked at them, and Una knew very well how they must look. She hadn't seen herself for more than a month, but she'd seen the other people on the ship, and she might well think the same thing of them.

"We will be just fine." Una said, trying to force herself to look stronger.

"Is the family traveling with us Irish too?" McKenna asked. This man was certainly Irish, though he barely had a lilt. McKenna thought that all his business was probably Irish as well.

"No. We'll be taking this family to California after we take you to Missouri."

"Where is California?" McKenna asked. Colin looked from McKenna to Una.

"Far out west. There's a rumor of gold out there. People can just pick it up off the ground and be rich."

Una watched McKenna's eyes grow wide, then leaned close to McKenna's ear. "He's just making a joke," she whispered.

The man stood up straighter. He said, "I'm not either. It's the truth."

Una nodded then took a breath, "I guess we'd better go find a place to stay then."

"We leave day after tomorrow at sunrise," Colin said, looking at a group of four horses a young boy was driving along the road.

Una held on tighter to her sister, "We'll be here."

Chapter Three

The girls found the boarding house they'd been recommended to. Everyone who stayed at the house was so poor that they all shared a large, single space. The floor was covered in mats. Each mat touched another mat, and every mat was accounted for. The women who boarded here slept in shifts. Many of the girls and women worked nearby but still could afford nothing else. Some, like Una and McKenna, were simply passing through and needed a place to sleep for the night.

The stern-looking woman who ran the boarding house pointed out the mat that the girl's would have to share.

That night Una curled around her sister and waited for sleep to come. It didn't. Thoughts of Boston, their journey, and their new life kept flowing through her mind, keeping her from sleep. Finally, her eyes closed in a drowsy haze. When she awoke, it was completely dark. She heard a rustle and thought it must be one of the other girls.

The sound came from close by and Una looked up into the darkness. As her eyes adjusted to a dim outline, she made the figure of a man.

"What are you doing?" Una asked loudly.

The figure froze.

Una sat up in time to see the man grab her dirty bundle and take off running. Realization overcame her. A few cries from sleeping girls rang out as the figure stepped on them. Una jumped to her feet and ran after him.

"Una!" She heard McKenna cry after her, but Una was moving fast. She jumped over the sleeping figures and around some of the girls who were now sitting up, watching what was going on. She flew out the door, down the hall, and out the front door of the boarding house.

Her bare feet hit the stone, and her legs felt rubbery, but she pushed forward anyway.

The figure hadn't expected her to come after him, and he'd slowed down but was still jogging ahead. Una moved faster and as silently as she could before ramming into him with all her might. She wasn't much, but she'd caught him off guard. The man tripped and fell to the ground. Her sack hit the ground, and she grabbed it with both hands.

Una looked down into the face of the man. His face went wide with surprise when he saw Una. He was working his way to his feet as if to grab the bag back, but Una pulled it in tight to her chest and kicked him low in the stomach.

"There's nothing you want here. I've no money and no food, so now you'll leave me be." She stood for a moment looking down at the man whose mouth opened as if to say something, but who was momentarily immobilized.

She turned and walked back, listening for sounds of feet or any indication of the man. There was none.

When she reached the door to the house, Una leaned against the inside wall and breathed a long, heavy sigh. When she walked back in, the room was in an odd state. Most of the girls were still sleeping, but a few were awake, calling out to one another, still trying to figure out what had happened.

Una went in feeling no compulsion to explain what had happened. She put the bag under her head and laid back down. She pulled McKenna in tight to her. Una brushed McKenna's hair with her fingertips until she felt her sister drop heavily into sleep. She knew there would be no sleep for her that night, so she stared into the darkness counting McKenna's breaths.

The next day, they were not allowed to stay in the boarding house because another wave of girls were coming in. These girls worked at night and slept during the day on the same mats in the same room. Una and McKenna roamed the streets of Boston with no money and no place to be. They stayed close by for fear their strength would give out and they would not be able to make it back to Mill Dam in time for their departure to Missouri.

Missouri was all Una could think about. Boston had become a place where she had to protect herself from thieves, where people were rude and unfriendly, and where her countrymen were still poor and hungry.

Una hadn't one more cent to spend on the boarding house so the two girls, exhausted and physically broken from such a day of walking, sat down where they'd first seen Seamus. They tucked themselves as far back from the street as possible to keep from being seen and becoming targets of some other night prowler. The night air had a nip to it. Neither girl slept. They talked in whispers about their upcoming trip, about the city they were in. There were far more people out on the streets at night than Una had thought there would be. Women walked to and from work unaccompanied. There were people huddled together in makeshift bedrooms. Every few minutes a horse could be heard clomping along the stone.

All of this surprised Una. In Ireland, out in the country, everyone woke up early and got to work before sunrise. In County Cork, no one had anywhere to be. There were no jobs and no farms to run. The only thing they'd been able to do was watch boats being loaded up with the last of the Irish produce to be shipped off to other lands, for other people to eat, while they themselves starved. Some people went crazy, and many died. Some slept all the time, balled up on the streets, in doorways, along the road.

Here, there was a flurry of activity. Una and McKenna stood as they saw Colin and Seamus approaching with their wagon. Una signaled a morning salute to Colin Hill.

"Morning to ya, glad to see you on time" His smile seemed significantly more chipper this morning than it had the other day when they'd first met.

Una saw a family of six standing on the other side of the road. They began moving toward them as the wagon appeared.

The family talked with Colin while Seamus took to loading their luggage and belongings into the wagon.

"Will you be taking them to California yourself?" Una asked Colin when he came toward them for her luggage—which, of course, was nothing.

Colin laughed, "No. They'll get their own wagon in Missouri and begin the real trip from there." Una nodded, looking them over again. They weren't Irish, Una could tell that right away, but beyond that she didn't know what they were. Just American, she assumed.

Though they didn't seem rich, they wore nice clothes with no holes, the wife wore a crisp bonnet, and the children had shoes that fit them. And they all looked well-fed.

Una looked at herself and her sister through their eyes. They were shabby, wearing clothing they'd been wearing for the last three years with holes showing everywhere. McKenna's feet had outgrown her own shoes, and she wore a pair of boy's shoes she'd taken from their middle brother after his death.

Their brother had been buried without shoes. The whole family was buried quickly, under only a few shallow feet of earth that McKenna, Una, and Kieran were already too weak to dig but had done anyway. It was one long grave. Their father lay next to their mother, and the other Brady children surrounded them.

The priest was long since dead from aiding the sick, so Kieran had said a prayer and a few words from the family Bible. The Bible was now one of the only things Una had not sold. She had it tucked into her sack.

Pressed between the front pages of the Bible were locks of hair from her dead family members. If she hadn't run after the man who'd tried to steal her sack, then even that would be gone. The man would have found the bag worthless and thrown it into the water. Una could not bear the thought of her last and only remnant from home finding its way to the bottom of the sea.

Well, we have nothing to be ashamed of, Una thought to herself as she looked the other family over. She must be strong for McKenna if not for herself.

It turned out that their Aunt Catherine had paid for the girls to have passage on the wagon and for their food along the way. At every meal, Una could feel the eyes of everyone on her and McKenna. Everyone could see clearly that they'd nearly starved to death, and that an intent, determined look entered their eyes when the food was being passed around.

Una took an even breath and began to eat just as she would if she were back home around her kitchen table. Soon, the other family began to eat, and no one showed any more interest in the eating habits of two Irish girls.

Each night they made camp, and each night Una and McKenna snuggled together under the night sky. It was amazing to Una how the sky was always there to greet her no matter where she was. They lay looking at the stars, finding constellations, finding their favorites, noticing when something had changed, until they fell asleep.

The air was different as they moved forward. It cleared. It felt more like the air at their old farm than the air of Boston or County Cork. Una often found herself taking deep breaths through her nostrils without even realizing it. When she did this, McKenna would giggle.

"You sound like a sow," McKenna would whisper.

Una laughed with her sister, "I don't mind that comparison at all. In fact, I take it as a very dear compliment. So thank you very much."

McKenna loved it when Una put on a very proper voice, and Una would do anything to make her sister smile these days.

The other family rarely talked to the girls, and Una could feel their wary disapproval in the way they looked at them. Una kept her thoughts on what lay ahead. She wondered if Catherine looked like their mother. She hoped that she did. She wondered if she was kind like her mother or if she would be upset with the girls for already costing her money.

Colin and his brother rode at the front of the wagon. And soon the entire group learned what the shiny object in Seamus' hand had been.

Seamus often walked out in front of the wagon to look for impediments to their journey, and as he went, he played songs on his harmonica. They were sweet songs. Some songs Una knew, some she'd heard as a child, and some she'd never heard before. Each one felt like a warm breeze. The group always grew silently sentimental when he played.

But Una's favorite part of the journey by far, was eating. They ate every day, twice. At first Una watched as McKenna put some of her food into her dress, keeping it for later. Later that night when they were unobserved, Una made McKenna eat all of it. She was malnourished enough without keeping important food from herself.

"There will be plenty of food from now on," Una said brushing her sister's cheek.

McKenna nodded her head not fully believing this. Una didn't blame her for that.

"I promise, okay?" Una smiled, and McKenna nodded.

Their arrival in St. Joseph, Missouri was anticlimactic. There was nothing different about this town from the countless others they'd passed through on their way here. They were in the town center, which seemed well established, but they'd travelled next to fields and open lands for miles on their way here.

"This is where everyone gets off," Colin said, hopping down from his perch on the wagon. His brother began to remove things from the wagon.

"What will you do now?" Una asked.

"We'll fill her up with things set for sale in Boston, split the money with the local folk around here who supply it, then bring another load of passengers back with us."

"Don't you get tired of travelling?" McKenna asked. Una had no doubt that her sister's body was bruised from the rough ride of the wagon just as hers was. Una took her sister's hand.

She spoke before Colin had time to answer her younger sister's question, "Do you know who Catherine Donnelly is? Would you know her if you saw her?"

Colin turned around in what was almost a full circle before stopping as his eyes settled on a woman walking toward them.

"There she is now."

Una looked at the woman then turned to Colin and said, "Thank you for everything."

"Good luck to you," he said, already focused back on his unloading.

Chapter Four

The woman walking toward them looked strong in a different way from their mother. She walked with a quick step. Her clothes were plain, a crisp bonnet covered her head, and her eyes squinted toward the girls. Una brushed out her dress and brought McKenna close to her.

When Catherine was just in front of them she opened her mouth to speak but no words came out. The girls studied Catherine as she, in turn, studied them.

Her face didn't look anything like their mother's face, and Una felt a disappointment lodge in her chest. She'd foolishly let her imagination run away with her.

"So you're Margaret's daughters," Catherine finally said. Una was surprised to hear an American voice speaking to her. There was no sound of the Irish blood she carried in her veins, in the trill of her speech.

"Yes, ma'am," Una said tilting her head down in deference to the older woman who had already helped them so much.

"Mama," yelled a young voice. It was a child's playful shout from a little boy who bounced into his mother's legs. He looked to be about six years old. He was followed by two older girls. They were certainly younger than McKenna, but because McKenna still looked so young, they appeared to be only a year or two younger when they were probably four or five years younger.

The children all stared at Una and McKenna wide-eyed and open-mouthed. They obviously hadn't expected their relatives to look so painfully poor. The girls had been able to scrub themselves since leaving the ship, but their clothes would never lose the putrid smell they had collected on their journey. With all their scrubbing, somehow they still looked dirty.

"Little Joe," Catherine put her hand on top of the little boy's head. "Sarah," she pointed to the eldest girl, "and Martha." Catherine turned her attention to her sister's daughters while giving each of her children a look of warning.

"This is McKenna and Una," Catherine matched up the wrong girl with the wrong name. Una cleared her throat the slightest bit and again bowed her head a bit in deference.

"Actually, ma'am, I'm Una, and this is my sister McKenna."

Una was surprised to see Catherine's cheeks turn a flush pink before correcting herself, "Of course you are."

"It's nice to meet you, Little Joe, Sarah, Martha," Una spoke to each in turn then McKenna did the same. The children still stared at the sisters with open mouths and wide, surprised faces.

"I can't say how grateful we are for all you've done for us. As soon as I can, I want to pay you back for the passage in the wagon."

Catherine nodded with an appraising look, "I appreciate that, but you are family, and now I believe I am your only family. Family takes care of its own. We worked out a barter with Mr. Hill. We had a good take for the last two years, so it all worked out quite well."

Catherine took a long breath. "We have a bit of shopping to do while we are in town. I think you both ought to pick out some new material for a new dress. We are not a rich family." Catherine opened her little purse and took out three coins and handed them to Una, "but the ones you are wearing won't do, and I don't suppose you have any others." This was more of a statement than a question, yet Catherine looked at the sack Una was carrying anyway.

"No, we don't. We have our family Bible and not much else." Una looked to the sack herself. Despite everything, Una was embarrassed to come so far with so little.

Catherine nodded.

"Sarah, Martha, will you take them to the store and help them find fabric?"

The eldest girl, who was probably twelve, nodded her head. She was looking with large eyes at Una, as if she were scared of being alone with such a person.

Una inhaled slowly and swallowed down what little pride she had left.

Catherine took Little Joe's hand and led him off at a quick clip toward a different side of the square.

Una took McKenna's hand, then released it, thinking that McKenna might not want to be treated like a child here.

As the group of four walked forward, every set of eyes that they passed fell on the sisters. They were so thin. What had been painfully commonplace in Ireland, even in Boston with so many Irish newly arrived, was strange here. This was a town where people had decent clothing, a bed to sleep on, and a hot meal three times a day.

From what Una could see, there was no one in such a poor condition as Una and McKenna. Una felt a powerful need to protect McKenna from the stares of those around them. She had to fight the urge to hide.

"This is where we'll get your things," Sarah said in a matter-of-fact tone that resembled one of a girl twice her age.

"Thank you," Una said awkwardly, as if the girl herself were the one paying for the material that would soon hide her immense poverty.

"You came from Ireland?" Maratha asked McKenna.

Maratha was probably no more than ten, and even though McKenna was sixteen, the ten-year-old felt her equal... and she was, in size.

"Yes," McKenna said.

"What is it like?" Maratha asked this like a girl who has been told of a place often enough that it has become almost mythical.

"Green, beautiful." McKenna's voice sounded far away. "It used to be perfect...."

Una could hear the unspoken, "But it's not anymore," and she was glad her sister hadn't said it.

"Our mother told us that everyone is dying there." Martha tilted her head at McKenna, probably thinking that these girls looked near death themselves.

McKenna nodded, and Una saw her eyes well up with tears. They hadn't cried. They had let a few tears fall a few times, but mostly they'd been too tired. Their survival had taken all of their energy. Now, having someone ask about it, the prospect of saying it out loud might have the power to crush McKenna. A little ten-year-old girl with more power than McKenna had ever had in her whole life.

"That's true," Una said. She pulled McKenna closer to herself and talked so her sister would not have to. "There is no food, so people are sick and starving."

The small troop of girls walked into the store with Sarah at the helm.

"Is that what happened to you? Were you starving too?" Martha asked, and Sarah gave her sister a warning nudge.

"I suppose we were, but now we have food, and because of your mother, we have much to be thankful for."

Martha beamed at this mention of her mother.

"Here it is," Sarah laid a hand across a ream of fabric. "You pick the one you want and then take it to the counter." Sarah pointed a finger to the counter where a woman was looking at Una and McKenna with distaste.

Sarah walked away from the fabric shelves with Martha in tow. Una watched them make their way to where the candy and toys were.

Una turned back to the reams of fabric, trying to ignore the feeling of the woman's eyes on her back.

"This one is lovely," Una said softly, letting her hand float across a dark green material. It felt creamy under her fingers.

The ream was suddenly taken from under her fingers. She looked up to see the woman who had just been at the front counter of the shop. The woman carefully placed the ream behind a small counter and turned back to Una, "I'm afraid this one is one of the more expensive materials. Let me find you something more in your price range."

Una felt her face burn hotly. Of course the woman was right, but it was something in the way she'd said it. The way she'd pulled the fabric away, as if Una's touch would make it dirty.

"I think that color would be perfect with that red hair," a man's deep voice came from behind Una.

She turned to find a man perhaps just under thirty with a ruddy complexion and a happy glow beneath his eyes. He smelled fresh and looked just as he smelled. Una wasn't sure if the glow in his eyes was meant to make fun of her or if it he was genuinely being nice.

Una lifted through her spine, trying to prepare herself for either eventuality.

"Good afternoon, Mr. Mackey," the woman's voice was tight, but she brought the green fabric back to the table.

"There now, let's see." The man lifted the fabric up and held it against Una's face. She watched his eyes, entranced by his easiness, his confidence. His face lit up as he looked between her face and the fabric.

"It's perfect, isn't it?" He turned to McKenna, who shone with delight at being asked.

"Perfect," McKenna agreed.

Una was transfixed by this strange apparition. Her heart was beating oddly, and she felt her palms growing sweaty. She'd not been the object of praise for longer than she could remember, and it left her at a loss for words or action. She tried to think, to tell her mind and body what she was supposed to do.

"No," Una said too loudly, flustered. "The lady is right, this fabric is certainly beyond my price range. I should be happy to see the other economical fabric, if you please." Una took the ream from the man's hands, and her hand skimmed his. He didn't flinch or pull away as she'd expected him to. Instead he seemed to hold the moment longer until Una put the fabric back on the counter.

"I would be happy to pay for it. It would be a crime to let you go on in a brown or grey, which I have no doubt Mrs. Wright was about to show you." His eyes danced. He was a handsome man, and Una had a feeling that he knew it. She couldn't decide if he was one of those superior young men who think they can bully and tease the rest of the world at will or the opposite. Her opinion of him could not find a resting place.

"There's nothing wrong with my brown or grey, they are all very high quality, I'll have you know, Mr. Mackey."

Una wanted to say something to the man, but she was unable. So, instead she turned to Mrs. Wright. "I will come back," Una said to the woman with as much conviction as she could muster. She'd never known buying fabric could be such a harrowing experience.

"No," The man grabbed her elbow and held her in place. "Please," He said in a soft, kind voice that Una was not prepared for. There was a momentary pause when Una, McKenna, the woman, and the man all looked at his hand on Una's elbow.

Quickly, he dropped it. "Please, don't let me keep you from your shopping. I was simply saying the truth, but I can see that I've made you uncomfortable. Please, let me be the one to go." He tipped his hat, which felt so strange to Una in her current circumstances that she almost wished him to treat her like the others seemed to be treating her.

She was unsure what to say, so she said nothing at all as she watched him leave the store.

Una turned back to the woman, who pressed her lips together and lifted her eyebrows. It was her first day in her new town and already Una felt an outsider.

"This is what I have," Una put the three coins on the counter where the woman had put the green fabric. "I need enough fabric for two dresses, one for each of us, and fabric for new undergarments and bonnets."

The woman looked at the coins and heaved out a sigh, but despite this she swiped them into her hand. She went to a shelf from which she pulled out a coarse brownish material and set it on the counter. She also got a rough linen that could be made into underclothes. With her new parcel tied up in hand, Una went over to where the two younger girls were picking out candies, handling each decision with the utmost import.

"I'll have these," Sarah said putting a small handful of candies on the counter. "And she'll have those," Sarah gestured to Martha who was setting her handful on the counter as well.

Una was surprised to watch Sarah pay for the candies out of a small purse of her own. Una pulled McKenna outside to wait for the girls there.

The sisters stood quietly outside of the store waiting for the two younger girls to come out. Una immediately looked around for the man but didn't see him anywhere. Since there seemed no danger of being surprised by the man, she let her mind wander to one that was already replaying in her imagination.

"He was right, you know," McKenna said looking up at her sister. Una looked down, not at all surprised that McKenna too, was still thinking of him.

"Right about what?"

"That color would look very good with your hair," she smiled, and Una smiled just from the sight of her sister smiling.

Once upon a time, the dresses that were now nearly falling off their bodies had been dyed bright colors. Una's had been pink, and McKenna's had been blue. Now they both looked a shabby, light gray with splotches of brown and yellow where stains had formed.

"Well, perhaps one day I will get it, and I will get you a gown of gold, plucked right from the California streets, and it will have puffed sleeves and be so shiny you will blind every suitor who falls in love with you. What do you think of that?"

McKenna smiled the way one smiles when they know something is impossible but still likes the idea of it anyway.

"No matter what," Una said. "We must remember where we've come from. We must remember that we are very lucky indeed. I do not require any green fabric, no matter how nice it is. I have you. We must be very thankful—"

"I am," McKenna said with a ferociousness that surprised Una.

Una nodded, "I know you are."

Chapter Five

With shopping done and the necessaries that the town had to offer in hand, the group's females plus Little Joe all got on the small family wagon and headed away from town.

Una thought that after today it would be okay with her if she never got on another wagon for the rest of her life. The younger Donnellys talked nonstop, teasing Little Joe with their candy from town, all the way out to the Donnelly farm.

"Alright, that will be enough chatter for one day," Catherine said when they pulled up to a small, plain farmhouse. The land around them was fertile and lovely. Una took a deep breath trying not to think of her family. Trying not to think of what life might be like if her whole family had left Ireland before the blight. If they had all come here together, rented a new farm, and planted food that grew perfectly healthy and made their bodies strong. Una shuddered at the thought and the longing that grew with it.

"You'll be staying with us until we can arrange your marriages," Catherine said in a perfunctory manner.

Marriages. Una had thought rarely about the men that awaited her and her sister on this side of the world. She'd only thought of safety, of food, the end of hunger, the end of sickness.

Now she thought of a husband.

There was a husband for her here. There was a husband for McKenna here. Una clutched at McKenna's shoulder. The sudden, overwhelming fear of her younger sister and only real family being taken away to a stranger's house folded in on her.

Of course they could not stay here with Catherine. The house was small. It was obvious that what she'd said in town, that the family was not rich, was true. They were not. They had enough, but that was all. Here in the Donnelly house, the Brady girls would be a burden. They would be taking important resources, had already done so by having the Donnellys pay or barter for the girls' passage from Boston to Missouri and for the new clothes that Una and McKenna would soon make from the parcel Una now carried.

Not only were they a burden, but they were also both still too weak to be of much help on the farm. Una tightened her jaw and made an immediate resolution that she would grow stronger, she would work hard, and that she would at least work hard enough that their stay with the Donnellys was not a complete loss to their family.

Una stood at the base of the wagon with McKenna as the rest of the family walked on toward the house. When Catherine realized they weren't following, she turned.

"Come along now. I'll show you where you are to stay." She waited until both girls moved before moving forward toward the house herself. "We don't have an extra bed, so Martha and Sarah will share, and you two girls can share." She said this without turning back to them. They walked into the house, and Una looked around.

The house was sparsely furnished, and everything was made of plain wood with very few flourishes or frills. It was very much like their old house in Ireland. Their house had been spare too, but with all the children, the noise, and all the love, it had seemed very full. This house did not have the same fullness about it. Una suspected that no house did.

"Una, perhaps you could help getting breakfast on the table, and McKenna, you could help with lunch and dinner."

"I can work on the farm in the fields after breakfast is made." Una said, though she understood Catherine to mean this even if she hadn't said so yet.

Catherine turned to Una and said, "Very good. McKenna can help the girls with the animals. In the evenings, we read the Bible, sew, and do any other work that can be done by the light of the fire before going off to bed."

Una looked into the main room. There was a kitchen, dinner table, fire, and chairs all in one room, and this made up the entire downstairs area.

Catherine began walking upstairs. Una followed her, but after only a few steps up, she felt the same restriction of breath she'd been feeling from exertion since she'd gotten off the ship. She tried to keep her breath sounding normal so Catherine wouldn't hear and think her incapable of pulling her own weight.

They walked into a tiny bedroom with two small beds, no fireplace, and a small washbasin. In the winter, the family must sleep downstairs near the fire.

"Martha and Sarah normally share this bed," Catherine pointed to a small bed nearest the window. "You two will share this one. This is normally Little Joe's, but he will sleep with us in our room for the time being," Catherine said, pointing to the other, equally small bed.

Una smiled. Small as it was, it was actually a good deal more space than they'd had when they were squeezed between strangers in the berths on the ship.

Una took a breath of relief. They were safe. This was what safety looked like. She set the fabric bundle onto the bed.

Mr. Donnelly was undoubtedly out in the fields doing work. The children had run off as soon as they'd come home, whether to do chores or to play, Una didn't know. Now, it was just Una and McKenna with Catherine watching them. Catherine sat back on the bed that her girls shared. By the look on the older woman's face, Una could see that Catherine wanted her to do the same.

Una sat on her new bed and gave McKenna a little touch on the arm to do the same.

"There are a few things I want to talk to you both about," Catherine said as she crisply folded her hands in her lap. "First of all, I would appreciate it if you kept some of the harsher details of what you've been through from the children. They understand that Ireland is in crisis, that people are starving, and I prepared them for—"

She stopped speaking, and Una knew that she meant she'd prepared them for the awful appearance she and McKenna might have on arrival. That they might look near death, that they would look dirty and poor. It was just as well that she had warned them. They certainly did look near death, poor, and dirty. Catherine did not finish her sentence but changed tracks.

"I thought it prudent to delay your meeting the men I've acquired for you both. Now, I see that I was right. I think it best that you get some rest, hard work, fresh air, and food in you before you are introduced."

What Catherine meant was that Una and McKenna were human scarecrows. They were so thin and so grotesque that no man would marry them if they were seen in these first days.

"When you do think that will be? That we are introduced?"

"I don't know," Catherine looked them over again. "I suppose we'll just have to wait and see—but the sooner the better."

The sooner the better for Catherine, Una thought. *Not for us.*

"…and…" Catherine said to McKenna, "you are… how old?"

Una had told Catherine in her letters, but Catherine seemed dubious, as well she should.

"Sixteen," McKenna said quietly.

Una spoke up. "McKenna stopped growing when the food began to run dry. I think she'll surprise all of us soon, once she gets a little food in her system."

Catherine smiled noncommittally at Una.

"Today, you should rest. We'll have to get those clothes off of you and give them a scrub as soon as possible," Catherine looked at their clothes. "Perhaps you can cut the material for your dresses tonight, wash, and get some good sleep. Tomorrow will be a new day."

Catherine stood to leave, and the two girls sat on the bed watching her go. Just before she stepped out of the door, she turned back to the girls.

"Perhaps you should cut the dresses large, give you each a bit of room to grow into them?"

Una nodded, "Yes, of course."

Then Catherine was gone, and once again, they were alone. The two sat quietly on the bed thinking of all that had happened and all they had seen since they'd arrived in St. Joseph.

"Do you think we'll like it here?" McKenna asked.

"Yes, I do," Una said, though she really wasn't at all sure. McKenna nodded her head, hearing what Una hadn't said.

She hadn't said that they ought to be happy to be alive. She hadn't said that though they ought to be happy for life, they may never be happy in life again. That there was no recovery from what they'd been through. That losing their entire family was enough to make Una wish she'd died too, that McKenna was the only reason she hadn't laid down on the side of the road next to Kieran and waited for death.

McKenna was her reason for living now, but neither girl would ever be the same. There was no going back now, and the road forward, though better than the one they'd walked coming here, would never really be theirs.

"When we get married, we will be split up?" McKenna asked. She was voicing what Una had been thinking since Catherine had mentioned it.

"No, not really. I will make sure of it. We will always be together." She pulled her sister in close to her and kissed the top of her head.

Though Una was only twenty herself and that left only a four-year age difference between the sisters, Una was really many years older than her sister.

"Like she said, we'll need to wash these," Una looked down at their dirty, threadbare clothes.

"Maybe we can just sew the others very fast," McKenna responded as she stared at what they were wearing.

That night at dinner, once again all eyes were on Una and McKenna. Una could not get used to the feeling of eyes staring at her while she was supposed to be eating. As if she might turn into an animal at any moment and rip apart her food with her teeth, piece by bloody piece.

She waited again for the other members of the family to begin. Only then did she begin herself with tiny, demure bites until she was satisfied that the curiosity of the family had been quelled.

"You'll have to eat more than that if you're to marry Saul Mackey," Said Joseph Donnelly at the far side of the table. "You're no bigger than a toothpick. He's liable to squash you flat on your wedding night," Joseph laughed loudly at his joke.

Catherine turned scarlet, "Joseph Donnelly, you'll not speak like that in this house." She said indignantly to her husband, who laughed even louder.

"I'll speak how I want in my own home, and I was only joking with the girl, wasn't I?"

"Squash her flat," Little Joe said repeating his father.

Joseph stopped laughing and turned to his son, "Now you're not to go repeating such things, eh?"

Little Joe sulked and pushed his fork into his plate of food.

Una and McKenna had just met Mr. Donnelly, but he acted as if he'd known them forever. When they'd first met, he'd patted McKenna on the head and given Una a pinch on the cheek.

He spoke to them with the same familiarity as one of their brothers.

"Well, aren't you two just skin and bones?" he'd said on first seeing them. Then he had walked over to the food being made and pulled a bit from each dish.

Now that the family had turned back to their food, Una thought about the Mr. Donnelly's words. He'd said "Saul Mackey," That was the name of the man she would marry, if everything went according to plan. Mackey, Una thought. She'd heard that name before. Mackey...

Una could feel McKenna's eyes on her, and she turned to her younger sister.

"The green dress," McKenna whispered to Una with a smile.

"What was that?" Joseph asked, not one to be left out of a conversation.

"I was just remembering a green fabric at the store, sir. That's all."

Joseph nodded, immediately letting go of the comment, since fabric and dresses were obviously a topic he did not care to talk or make jokes about.

Una cut into her food. The green dress. Una stopped moving. The man. That's what the woman had said, hadn't she? Mackey? Mr. Mackey? McKenna had heard it too.

Was that possible? Had she met her future husband without even knowing it? And if she had, then had he known it? He would have had to. This town wasn't that big, and Una and McKenna stood out like a sore thumb. There was certainly no way two rail-thin, young women in bedraggled clothing with two Donnelly children nearby could escape the obvious conclusions to their identity.

Una's heart sank. He was handsome. So handsome... and she was... she looked terrible, and she knew it. If only it could have been a different day. If she could at least have been in her new dress, even if it were coarse. No man in farming country would want a skeleton for a wife.

Una looked around the table. Soon he would come and tell Joseph that she was not marriage material. He would say he wanted to call it off, and all before she'd been able to say one real word to him.

McKenna squeezed her hand under the table. Una could tell that McKenna wanted to say something more, but Una shot her a warning look. There would be no more talking in audible whispers at the dinner table.

Chapter Six

As the first weeks went by, there was no word from Saul Mackey, no word that he wanted to call it all off, that he'd seen Una and changed his mind.

She'd been anticipating a knock, a whispered word between Catherine and Joseph, or some other telltale sign, but none came.

Una ate as much as she could without taking more than her share, and she made sure McKenna ate every bite of her food as well. Even after one week, the girls were beginning to look and feel better. Una pushed herself hard in the fields, lifting things, walking as fast as she could, trying to gain some of her old strength back. She could tell that it would take a long while, but she could also feel the shadow of her former self waking up under her skin.

McKenna began to grow vertically almost immediately. Each time Una saw a small difference in her sister, it made Una's heart lift.

After two months, Una began to wonder how long it would be before she was officially introduced to Saul. Una worked hard to pull her hair back in an attractive manner, and kept her fingernails clean, even with all the field work she was doing each day.

One evening when Una was coming in, Catherine and McKenna came rushing out to meet her.

"You need to go in and get cleaned up. I've put one of my dresses on your bed. You're to wear that this evening."

"Why?" Una's heart beat faster, but she didn't need an answer to know why. She understood very well what was about to happen. Without waiting for an answer from Catherine, Una practically ran inside. The last thing she needed was to look as terrible as she had the first time. She had to be at her best now.

Every night before she went to bed she'd been thinking of Saul and his green eyes, his dark hair, his nicely curved face, and strong shoulders. She wasn't sure if he'd been growing more handsome, less handsome, or the same in her mind, so she promised herself to keep her expectations to a minimum.

Una ran upstairs and pulled off her dress. She began to scrub her neck and face and hands. She rubbed the skin until it was almost red and raw, then picked up the dress that was laid out on the bed.

"It's him, it's him!" McKenna came running into the room, and Una put a finger up to her mouth. "It's him," McKenna whispered to Una once more, and Una smiled. They walked quietly to the window of the room, and Una slipped a finger under the white linen curtain that covered it. She pulled the curtain free an inch and looked out.

Stepping out of a carriage was the man she'd met at the store. He was even more handsome than she'd remembered him. She watched as his feet hit the ground and he spoke in a light tone to Joseph. Suddenly his eyes flicked up to the window and locked with Una's.

Una gasped and let the curtain drop back into place. She put her hand over her mouth and looked at her sister.

They both began to laugh silently to one another. Una looked down and saw that she was in her under things and laughed some more, hoping to the heavens that he hadn't been able to see anything beyond her face.

She picked up the dress, and McKenna helped her into it.

"Wash your hands and your face," Una commanded her sister, then looked at herself in the mirror. The dress was too big. Much too big, but at least she'd gained some weight in the last month. Her face was no longer haunted, no longer so skeletal that each one of her bones was visible.

McKenna finished scrubbing while Una combed out her hair and pulled it into a clean, flattering style on top of her head. She pinched her cheeks and smiled at herself, trying it out. It would have to do.

"Wait," McKenna said pulling a sash out of one of Sarah's dresses and tying it around Una's waist to give her shape. It helped.

Una nodded, "Good thinking."

As they walked out of the room, Una let McKenna go first, since McKenna was anxious to get downstairs into the interesting parts of the evening, and Una was almost paralyzed with fear.

She walked unsteadily down the steps, her heart hammering out a tune that ran the full length of her body.

As she came down the steps, she first saw two boots, then a pair of trousers, a shirt and jacket that stretched across a broad chest, then the beautiful face she'd seen so many times before she'd gone to sleep.

It was better than she'd remembered.

Her eyes met his green eyes and burned there before she turned them to the floor in embarrassment. When she stepped down the final step, Catherine looked at her happily and stepped forward.

"Una, I would like you to meet Saul Mackey," Catherine said as she held a hand aloft. Una had to look again, because Catherine was pointing to someone Una hadn't even noticed. A large, burly man with a thick, reddish-brown beard. His nose was stubbed and his front tooth chipped. He looked hard and serious, towering over them all. He was at least twenty years Una's senior.

Una caught her breath, aware that she was being introduced to this man and was now being rude.

"I," She stammered. "It's nice to meet you."

He didn't say anything but nodded his head in greeting then picked at his hat, which was clenched in his two large hands.

"This is Saul's brother, Henry." Now Catherine opened her arm in the direction of the man Una had been thinking about since the day she'd met him in town.

"It's nice to officially meet you," Henry nodded his head in her direction with a twinkle in his green eyes.

"You as well," Una felt her face grow hot and turned her gaze to the floor.

McKenna was also introduced, and the group was escorted to seats. They sat around the fire talking before dinner. Unfortunately Henry and Joseph seemed to be the ones doing the majority of talking.

Una found herself equally absorbed by Henry and trying not to be. She was thankful when it was time for dinner. There wasn't space for them all so the children had to eat separately, and they were still crowded in around the table.

Una thought that dinner would be easier, but it seemed just the same. She'd hardly heard two words out of Saul's mouth and could barely identify if he had a real voice or not.

Suddenly she looked over and found Henry looking at her. He tried to shift his eyes a bit but not before she'd seen his intense gaze.

"Mackey is Irish isn't it?" Una asked this of Saul who nodded his head the smallest amount and looked at his brother who took over. This seemed to be their usual method of doing things. Una wondered what Saul did when Henry wasn't around.

How did he communicate with the outside world? Or even, did he communicate with the outside world?

"Yes, we're a few generations back, though. No family there anymore." Henry looked at Una. "We're all so sorry for what's going on there."

Una nodded.

"I still can't believe we're here. That we are alive." McKenna said in a far-off voice that worried Una. It was unlike her sister to talk that way and especially to strangers. But, perhaps her sister felt as Una did that she already knew Henry.

"Gone," Una said. "They were taken all at once with sickness."

There was silence at the table, and Una remembered what Catherine said about talking in front of the children. But they were upstairs or outside.

"We were a good family before that. The best," McKenna said, again in that faraway voice that made Una look at her hard. "With a good farm. Our father's name was Owen, and he could dance like you couldn't believe."

Una laughed with tears in her eyes, "He could, too."

"Our mother never had a sour day in her life," McKenna continued.

"Well, I wouldn't say she never did. There were times, when Father drank too much," Una looked at Catherine who looked slightly horrified at this. "Or when he sang early in the morning and woke everyone in the house up."

McKenna moved closer to Una.

"Anyway," Una said trying to let the heaviness that had just fallen over the table go. "It's all so sad, not something to talk about at the dinner table."

"It's good to talk," Henry said. Una looked up at him and saw her pain reflected back at her through his eyes. "Talking heals, it keeps them alive. They deserve that… you deserve that." He looked to McKenna too, who had two streaks of tears rolling down her cheeks.

Una reached over and rubbed one cheek free of them.

Saul and Henry both produced handkerchiefs at the same time, and Una turned into them, forced to choose between the two.

She smiled faintly at Saul and took his proffered piece of white cloth then moved to McKenna as her eyes shifted swiftly to Henry.

Chapter Seven

It had been four days since their dinner with the Mackeys, and Una's head was still tumbling. It all made perfect sense now. Of course, Henry would easily find a wife. He would want to pick his own. Henry would certainly not let himself be subjected to an arrangement, not a mail-order bride.

Saul, on the other hand, was the perfect candidate for such an arrangement. He had just inherited his farm after the death of his father. He would be wanting children, a line of boys who would inherit after him. He was shy, taciturn, and awkward. He had none of the charming characteristics his brother had.

In fact, the only thing they seemed to share was their name. Mackey.

After they'd left, Catherine had told Una and McKenna about the Mackey family. Henry was the youngest and the last to settle down with a wife and start his own farm. Saul was the oldest and had just inherited. The two brothers had lived together alone for the last year since their father's death.

Henry appeared to be in no hurry to get to the altar, but Saul's marriage would be just the thing to spur him on. This seemed to be the town's stance on things, and there was a nice line of women awaiting Henry when that time came.

Catherine wanted to know Una's thoughts about Saul, and Una tried to placate her as best she could.

She tried to like him. Wanted to like him. She was trying to find qualities that she liked, there must be some, probably quite a few, but how was she to ever find them out if he never spoke? He was so incredibly quiet.

Then there was Henry. She was so disappointed that Henry wasn't the Saul she'd heard about that it was hard to look at Saul as anyone but the man who wasn't Henry.

But she must, she knew she must. She had to push forward and make the best of this. Saul would turn out to be a very nice man, she was sure. She had to let go of her evening reveries and turn instead to a new reality.

Even McKenna seemed disappointed that Saul was Saul and Henry was Henry.

McKenna's nightmares seemed to be growing worse since their dinnertime talk about their family. She would wake in the night in a panic of sweat, screaming and crying. Most of the time this woke the whole house up. She would often wake up quickly and be able to wake her sister and murmur to her until she fell asleep again. It happened multiple times a night, and Una, as well as the rest of the family, seemed to wear a new sleepy patina to their days.

Una had decided that a nice long walk sometime during the day might help. Maybe a little exercise and fresh air would help, some time alone with her sister away from chores just to clear out her head. Maybe that would help.

On their first day, they'd decided that if Una and McKenna took a very quick lunch they would have enough time to go for their walk before coming back to the their second half of the day.

On their second day, they decided to move their walk to the evening after dinner. The sun was still out enough for them to see, and there was a calm in the air that they both appreciated.

As they approached a knobby tree, the girls decided to sit by it for a moment and listen to the sounds of the evening. Una sat with her back against the thick trunk that felt strong and immovable behind her. McKenna picked little flowers from the grass and wove them together to make a necklace. This seemed to Una to be an arduous task with little payoff, but it relaxed McKenna, so she encouraged the activity.

"Will you make me one too?" Una asked as she watched her sister's small fingers moving the stems together until they were joined.

"Here," McKenna took off the necklace she'd already made and handed it to her sister.

"No," Una put up a hand. "I want one to match yours, so we both have one."

McKenna smiled and put her necklace back around her neck, continuing on with her task.

A deep patter of horse hooves beating down on the dirt road began from the west. Both girls looked in the direction the sound was coming from. McKenna looked back and forth from the direction of the sound, down to her necklace in progress. Una looked out, half watching and half distracted by the dusky look of the sky.

When the rider came into view, Una sat up and McKenna stopped making her necklace.

"It's Henry," McKenna said, putting her flowers into the lap of her dress. Una nodded but didn't say anything, watching as the figure came closer.

As Henry approached, he slowed down to a trot and then to a walk. He smiled at both the girls.

"Hello to the Brady sisters."

Una smiled lightly, and McKenna smiled with unabashed favor.

"I'm making flower necklaces. One for Una, and then I can make you one if you like?"

Henry swung his leg over his saddle and jumped down from his horse, "How could I pass up an offer like that?"

He walked over and sat next to McKenna as she finished Una's necklace, handed it over, and began a fresh one for Henry.

Una said, "If I didn't know better, I would say you are making that one with much more care than the one you made me."

McKenna looked up at Una and rolled her eyes, "I know you love me, so you will wear it even if it is not so good. Henry can throw his away whenever he likes so I have to make it especially good so he won't."

"Very good logic," Henry nodded with approval. "But, if I promise not to throw it away, will that help?"

"Quite," McKenna said. "Now, I can make it as sloppy as I like."

Henry laughed, and Una listened to the sound. It made her catch her breath, it was so honest and unencumbered.

"So, my dear ladies, what have you been up to?"

"Well," Una said. "I baked a loaf of bread to go with breakfast."

"Tough work indeed. I tried to make bread once, when my mother was alive. I had no idea how difficult a project it would be."

"And how was the bread?" McKenna asked.

"Terrible, like a rock. No one would eat it, not even the animals."

"Tsk," Una gave a mocking reprimand. "It really is not so difficult."

"Some might say it's easy," McKenna said with a dainty smile before turning back to her necklace.

"You ladies sure know how to put a fellow in his place," he said, pretending to brush off his wounded pride, then smiling widely at Una.

The three sat in amiable silence for a few minutes. Una looking off into the sky, McKenna's hands weaving small white bulbous flowers together, and Henry with his eyes closed soaking it all in.

"Catherine says that you'll be getting your own farm soon," McKenna said out of the quiet.

Henry looked at Una then leaned back to look into the branches of the tree.

"Yes, I've been looking, I suppose. When Saul—" He trailed off without finishing the thought. "One of these days, I will have to find my own place, my own land. I just… I guess I've been putting it off."

"Why?" McKenna looked up and held out Henry's brand new necklace.

"It's beautiful." He took the necklace and put it over his neck. "I can wear this with all my best gowns."

McKenna laughed, and Una noticed that he hadn't answered her question.

"I should get this to a safe place," Henry said, standing up. At once a frown fell over McKenna's face. "You, my dear, have nothing to be upset about," he said to McKenna. Henry said, "I was just told by a little birdie that there is a surprise waiting for you when you get home."

"A surprise?"

"That's what I heard."

Una looked at Henry's face carefully.

"What sort of surprise?" McKenna asked. The anticipation was oozing out of her.

"If I told you that then it wouldn't be a surprise, now would it?"

McKenna seemed to accept this and stood abruptly. Una could see the determined look in her sister's face and was about to stand up when Henry reached a hand out to help her. Una looked at the hand and then at its owner. She took it, her eyes never leaving his as he helped lift her to her feet. His hand was warm in hers. His skin was a mixture of soft and rough, the usual patches of worn skin that appeared on every farmer's hands. Hers included.

Una stood with her hand in his, only a foot between them for what felt like far too long.

"I really should go," his voice was softer, and Una carefully pulled her hand away.

"We should too," Una said as she looked to McKenna who'd already begun walking toward the house. McKenna turned back.

"Come on, Una." She gave her sister a pleading glance and a wave of her hand.

Una looked at Henry and said, "Well, you've certainly got her moving."

He nodded with a smile. He looked into Una's eyes for a burning moment. Una opened her mouth just as Henry began to turn to his horse.

He turned back abruptly, "What?" His face was earnest.

"Nothing." She was surprised at the voracity of his interest.

"You were about to say something...." He waited. "Please, say it."

"Just," Una swallowed and looked at her sister's frame walking along the road. "When I first met you, the woman at the store called you Mr. Mackey."

"Yes." He didn't say this as a question but as a confirmation, and she tilted her head at him. "And, you thought that I...?"

"That you were, that you were the one I was supposed to marry." She tried to say it on a laugh, but it got caught in her throat somewhere. Henry's eyes were paralyzing.

"Would you have liked that?" He was serious, his brow furrowed, his body tense, on the verge of something.

Una couldn't answer. How could she answer? She felt her face go hot and her heart pick up.

When she opened her mouth again Henry had moved. His lips came to hers, breathing in her unspoken words. His hand went to her face, his body pulling in to hers. She felt the world drop away from her, then just as quickly as it had begun, it was over.

They were apart, staring at one another. Breathing heavily. The weight between them so heavy.

"I'd better go," she said, pointing rather than looking in the direction of her sister.

He nodded and watched her for a moment more with some thought, some unknown thought moving through his mind, reflecting something she didn't understand on his face. Finally he turned and mounted his horse. He gave Una one last look before speeding off in the opposite direction from which he'd come.

She watched Henry's horse create a cloud of dirt, then turned toward her sister, who was marching along paying little heed to her sister's progress.

Una had to run to catch up to her little sister's march forward.

"Thank you for my necklace," Una said trying to clear her mind of Henry and make room for him at the same time.

McKenna turned to her sister, stopping mid-stride.

"There is something about Henry. Isn't there?" She said. Una could feel her sister trying to prompt her into talk, but Una didn't trust herself to say anything more than what her sister had just said.

Una adjusted her sister's necklace of flowers, "Yes, there is something about Henry." Una exhaled slowly. That was all she could say. Even that was too much. For McKenna, this was enough. She turned and began her march home again.

When they walked up to the farmhouse, McKenna began looking around for things that could be construed as surprises, but she found nothing. The girls walked into the house, and still nothing met their eye.

The family was sitting by a small fire, reading. Una walked in to sit with them, and McKenna reluctantly did the same. They sat with an uncomfortable sense of misunderstanding gnawing at the back of both their minds.

It wasn't until the evening reading was over, Catherine was collecting her sewing, and the children were climbing up the stairs that Catherine turned Una.

"Oh, there's something for you, in your room. Henry brought it by," she said, smiling at Una. Una tried not to smile, unsure what Catherine was suggesting. "I think it's from Saul."

Now Una smiled as well. She walked calmly up the stairs with McKenna in tow. When they got into the room and found the two younger girls running out with a dispute for their mother to settle, Una looked to the bed.

Sitting on top of the cover were two small packages wrapped in brown paper. One was labeled "M" and the other "U."

Una sat on the bed and handed McKenna hers, knowing her sister was dying to see what was inside. She ripped the paper with small, serious little rips, trying to keep it as intact as possible and finally opened the paper wide.

A large assortment of candy from the store peered back up at her. Within the candy there also sat a wooden game McKenna used to play in Ireland. Una could feel the breath of happiness go in and out of her. McKenna picked up a piece of candy and immediately put it in her mouth, then offered one to her sister.

Una smiled. "No, those are for you, you should enjoy them."

McKenna held the toy and put the rest of the candy away with some cloth so the younger children wouldn't find it and get into it.

"Now yours," McKenna said, her mouth turning red from the candy.

Una laughed at her sister's enthusiasm.

"I should let you open this," Una said, but she didn't hand the parcel over.

As she peeled back the brown paper, her heart stopped for a moment. She let her hand roam over it. Then, slowly, she pulled out a long sheath of perfect, dark green fabric.

Chapter Eight

The fabric was soft and supple under Una's fingers as she sewed along the line she'd created for her pattern. The fabric was more beautiful than anything she'd owned in Ireland, even when the harvests had been good and there was food and money to spare.

It was late, and the family was sitting by the fire. Una and McKenna were both sewing. The younger girls were taking turns reading the Psalms aloud. Little Joe was feeding the fire and stoking it with vigor. Catherine was darning stockings, and Joseph was asleep in his chair, occasionally waking up with a start from the sound of his own snores.

"Prosperity," Sarah said, correcting her sister's pronunciation.

"Prosperity," Martha repeated with pressed lips. "Let the light of your face shine on us."

Una smiled at the younger girls. They were sweet girls who had seen very little suffering in their lives. It was the way children were meant to be.

Una pushed her needle through the fabric. Her fingers were calloused from the work she was doing during the days. She worked as hard as Joseph did and harder than Catherine. She was so determined to make herself useful, to help justify their presence in the household. Her body was sore every single day. She ate well but tried to eat no more than her share. Still, she was gaining weight and so was McKenna. Their figures were filling out, their skin was shining, their hair was becoming thick and supple again, and their eyes were far less haunted than they had been.

"Ok, that will do for tonight." Catherine said. Joseph woke up once more and looked sleepily into the fire.

"I want to stay," Little Joseph looked up from his fire-stoking pursuits.

"No, it's time for bed now." Catherine stood, and Martha happily slammed the Bible closed, running it back to its dedicated spot on a small shelf.

"Come along," Sarah held out her hand to her younger brother. Her tone was matronly. She'd learned to boss her siblings around with great solemnity. Una pushed her needle into her fabric and began to collect her things.

"Una," Catherine said, "Saul is coming to dinner tomorrow night."

Una paused, then nodded. It would be foolish for her to ask about Henry, but the questioned burned in her mind, wanting to be answered.

"I was thinking that you should stay in from the fields after lunch tomorrow. You can help me make dinner. It will be good to show Saul that you can cook."

"Yes, of course." Una said.

Una and McKenna walked upstairs after Martha and Sarah had already gone up.

"Maybe Henry will come," McKenna whispered to her.

Una gave McKenna a little squeeze to her arm. *Maybe he would*, she thought.

~

The next day, Una went out before the sun was up to begin work on the farm. She wanted to get as much done as she could before lunch. Her back was sore from the day before, and her feet and the pads of her hands had new blisters.

The day dragged on. Joseph was quiet, and the younger children barely made any noise, leaving Una in her head for most of the day.

She kept remembering Henry's lips on hers. Her heart would thunder, her body shiver and she would look around, thinking that anyone watching must certainly know exactly who and what she was thinking about.

By mid-day, she'd given up trying to control her mind and had given herself over to the imaginings of her brain. The feel of his fingers touching her, his face so close to hers that she could see every mark, so close that she could taste his breath, the way his eyelashes framed his eyes in the dimming light.

When lunch finally arrived, Una was too excited to eat anything. She tried to pull her mind away from thoughts of Henry but found herself floating off over and over again.

"Una?" Catherine broke through her consciousness.

"Hm?" She wasn't sure if she'd just been asked a question.

"She's excited to see Saul tonight," Sarah said. Martha giggled. Una realized that she must have been lost in thought with a smile on her face.

"I asked if you know how to cook mutton?" Catherine smiled too, and Una blushed.

"Yes, that should be fine."

~

Dinner was boiled mutton, currant jelly, and a mutton broth soup with vegetables. Catherine showed Una how to make an apple pie for dessert, and the whole house smelled wonderful by the time Una cleaned up for dinner.

The children ate early and were sent out as soon as the wagon was heard outside.

"Henry," Catherine said as the younger brother came in first, "how's the farm?"

"Quite well, ma'am, thank you for asking."

Henry turned his eyes on Una, and she felt a searing heat rise in her.

Saul lumbered in behind his brother, and his eyes also turned to Una. Una grew redder with the heat of both brothers' eyes on her at once.

"Una has prepared our dinner for this evening," Catherine said straight to Saul. Saul seemed embarrassed by this. Una looked away from both of the brothers.

"Why don't we sit down and eat? I think you will both be surprised by Una's skill in the kitchen," Catherine said as she guided everyone to the table.

"It smells good," Saul said in a low almost inaudible voice.

"What?" Una leaned forward.

Saul didn't say anything, and Una looked to Henry.

"Saul is right, it does smell good," Henry said. He seemed ready to step in to help his brother in a way that suggested he'd done it many times before. A sinking feeling fell over Una. Saul was here for her.

Una was happy to be serving the dinner. Catherine had really done quite a bit of the cooking herself, but she left this fact out every time she talked about the food. She also talked about how useful Una was and how she worked hard on the farm, how Una would do well as a farmer's wife, "one day very soon."

Catherine's comments made Una feel like she was being physically pushed toward Saul and the altar.

When Una sat down and everyone was around the table eating dinner, there was an awkward break in speech. Una could think of nothing to say herself, Saul didn't really speak, Henry was deferring to the others, and Catherine had run out of topics that would get Una to the altar faster. It probably would have been easier if the children had stayed for dinner. They would at least think of something to talk about.

There was the general sound of food being consumed, and Una bit her lip trying to think of something that might be of interest to the table at large.

"Are you all going to the dance next week?" Henry looked up from his plate right into Una's eyes. She blushed.

"Yes, Horace Boucher is coming to take us. We haven't met him yet but—" Una broke off. Horace had been obtained as McKenna's intended, and Una wasn't sure how to say this. "He's taking us," she finished lamely. "Do you know him?"

Una had been trying to get more details about Horace from Catherine since they'd arrived, but Catherine hadn't said any more about Horace than she wanted to. Una had heard that he was something of a wealthy landowner, but that was it. Catherine seemed to think this the only important fact.

"Yes, not well, but in a town this size, you know everyone," Henry nodded. "It was a tragedy about his wife. She was in a carriage accident, died immediately, they say. Just last winter it was. Left Horace with three little ones to take care of. They can't be over six years old."

"And he has been taking care of them and his farm all by himself?" Una asked.

"No, he has help with both." Henry took a forkful of mutton and chewed it while thinking. "I think it's his sister who is living with him to help take care of the children, and he has always had help with the farm. It's too much land for one man to manage alone."

Una nodded. She wanted to turn and look at her sister, but she could feel her sister's worry easily enough without looking.

"McKenna, will you help me with the pie?" Una asked. She wanted to give McKenna some time to pull herself together, to think about something else.

The two girls pulled back from the table, and Una sliced the pie, putting each piece on a plate while McKenna walked them around to each person.

"The dance will be good fun, they always are. Even the local minister dances." Henry smiled brightly as he said it.

"*And* drinks liquor," Catherine said with a bite of disdain.

"Catherine, everyone is allowed to relax every once in a while, aren't they?" Henry smiled at her.

"The good Lord doesn't relax, so I wouldn't think a minister would either."

Una took a bite of the pie. It was very good. Catherine had stood over her the whole time making sure she did everything in the right order. Her family had never made or eaten pies. They'd had spice cake or pudding if they wanted something special.

"I think last time someone played a jig," Henry said, and his eyes flicked back to Una.

"Really? How do people normally dance around here?" Una asked.

"Not like the Irish. You'll just have to try your best to keep up… or slow down as it may be."

"Is there usually a fiddle?"

Henry nodded, "Yes. I daresay you'll have a few good tunes to dance to. There will probably be some dances you've never seen before that you will need to learn." He paused, "In fact, I can teach you if you like."

Una felt all the eyes at the table shift to her.

She knew what she was supposed to say, knew it would be a good time to turn to Saul, but she didn't.

"Perhaps," she said as she nodded just the least bit. Then she looked back to her pie and took another bite.

"Saul, do you dance?" Catherine asked. Una's eyes moved to Catherine, then to Saul. Each person quickly looked at Una, then looked away. Una exhaled slowly.

"Very little," Saul said in his quiet way. Una wanted to shout at him to speak up. She could barely hear him.

"Perhaps *you* can teach Una a few as well," Catherine looked at Una pointedly.

The look was not lost on Una. Una looked to Saul and could imagine herself repeating Catherine's request. Her imagination could clearly see what was wanted from her in the situation, but her lips would not move.

Saul gave a grunt and a half-nod before lifting the rest of his pie into his mouth.

Chapter Nine

"What do you think he'll be like?" McKenna said as she stood in her underclothes looking out of the window at the fields.

"You'll have to get dressed if you're ever to find out," Una said as she looked over the stitching on McKenna's dress. She held it up for her sister to step into. McKenna turned toward her and walked forward. She seemed hesitant, and Una couldn't help but worry for her sister. Catherine had told them none of what Henry had added to their picture of Horace Boucher. Was Catherine worried that it would repel McKenna, or did she know it wasn't the best of situations to be going into?

Una wanted to know all about him, but they would both find out soon enough.

The town dance would start in a little over an hour, and Horace was coming to pick the two girls up. Catherine and Joseph were going on their own to give Horace a chance to get to know McKenna.

"What if I don't like him?" McKenna asked. "What will happen then?"

"Don't worry, we'll figure it out. If you don't like him, then you don't have to marry him."

McKenna looked into Una's eyes, and Una felt that her sister could sense her own uncertainty.

Una didn't know what power she had or what she could really do if McKenna didn't like the man coming to get them. In the same way, there was nothing she could really do about Saul. Saul wasn't what Una dreamed of, but what choice did she have? She couldn't disgrace Catherine after all that Catherine had done for her.

There was also Henry to think of. Henry could hardly just trade his brother for Una. Saul was his family, and Una had no idea what their relationship was like. She didn't suppose it was anything as close as her relationship with McKenna. Saul was the oldest of the family, and Henry was the youngest. With Saul's quiet ways, it was hard for Una to imagine him being close with anyone at all.

"Do you think Saul talks when he's at home?" McKenna asked. Una looked up at her quickly, wondering how she'd picked up her own thread of thought so easily.

"I don't know. He is quiet, isn't he?"

"He barely says anything at all. Won't that get boring for you?"

Una ran a hand over her own hair and straightened out her dress. "Yes, I believe it might," she said. She smiled, but McKenna didn't smile back.

"I'm afraid." Suddenly McKenna seemed like a child the age of Martha again. She wasn't ready for this. Not for marriage to a man with three children and a dead wife.

"I'm sorry," Una brushed her fingers across McKenna's cheek. "Try not to be afraid, not tonight. We will just meet this Horace as if he's just going to be our friend, okay?"

McKenna nodded but didn't say anything.

Both girls put small flowers in their hair. Una thought that they both might just look more beautiful than they had in years, if ever. McKenna's hair was a lighter red than Una's, and both girls finally had curves to their faces.

"Don't you both look lovely," Catherine held each by the shoulders while she looked them over. "You are lucky to have a man who thinks of such things," Catherine said of the green fabric. Una wondered if Catherine really thought that Saul had been the one to think of the fabric. Did she really think Saul capable of such displays when he could hardly say hello?

"Yes, I am." Una said thinking of Henry as she said it.

There was a knock on the door, and all the motion in the foyer seemed to halt at once. McKenna's face turned white. Una wanted to reach out a hand to protect her sister, but Catherine was standing directly between them.

"Well," Catherine turned to McKenna, "why don't you get the door?"

McKenna blushed scarlet and walked to the door. Una could see her sister's hand trembling. She reached up and opened the door.

A large figure took up most of the doorframe.

Catherine moved forward, but to Una, it felt like Catherine was nervous around the man as well.

"Horace, come in," Catherine motioned. McKenna stood back and looked to the floor.

The large man walked in, and Una looked him over. He was well dressed and had a moustache and a wry smile. The thing that bothered Una was how old the man looked. He was certainly more than double McKenna's age.

"Horace," Catherine stepped back, "this is McKenna Brady."

Horace looked McKenna over in the way a person might look at a cow they were thinking of buying. He obviously didn't feel rushed or awkward because he took his time and took no pains to hide his observations.

"Good to meet you," Horace said after a long while.

When Una looked at McKenna again, she could see that her sister was trembling. McKenna gave a little curtsey and said, "You as well, sir." Horace smiled after McKenna spoke.

"This is McKenna's sister, Una." Catherine said after Horace seemed to be done with his introductions to McKenna.

Horace turned his cool blue eyes on Una, and she had to quell the urge to tremble as well. He nodded at Una, and Una nodded back in recognition.

"Joseph is just finishing up outside, he should be in soon," Catherine said. The group stood looking at one another.

Una shifted, "Are you very fond of dancing, Mr. Boucher?"

Horace turned his eyes back to her, and she saw a twinkle there that she didn't quite understand.

"Yes, I'm never opposed to a good bit of music. What about you and your sister?" He looked at McKenna. "Do you do much in the way of dancing?"

McKenna's eyes grew wide. "When we can," Una said quickly. "I'm afraid we may not know many American dances."

Horace nodded.

"I suppose we'll get on our way," Horace said abruptly. He turned back toward the front door, and Catherine hastened to follow.

"Yes," Catherine said. "No need to wait for Joseph. We'll see you there."

Una went to McKenna's side, and the children flanked them the moment the girls stepped outside.

"I like your carriage," Little Joseph said to Horace. The children must have been waiting outside while Horace was in the house. Una had to admit that the carriage was lovely. It was nicer than anything the Donnellys owned and probably nicer than anything else they'd seen yet in St. Joseph.

Horace helped McKenna up, and Una watched him take her sister's hand as he did. He then helped Una up so that McKenna would be sitting next to Horace as they drove and Una would be sitting on McKenna's other side.

Little Joseph ran after the carriage for a few minutes as they left, but soon they were out in the silence of the large fields. Horace didn't try to start up any conversation, so Una decided not to try and talk to him just yet. There was a lot she wanted to know, but his silence came as something of a relief. Why was it that this man made them all nervous?

After the story, neither girl had anything to say. The conversation died away again. When they began to see other wagons and townsfolk coming into town on foot, Una kicked herself for not making the best of the opportunity. There was a lot she wanted to know about this man, and there was no reason for her to be moved to silence by him.

Somehow, without Una's realizing it, the group of three went the entire trip without a real conversation growing between them. They had talked briefly about the fields they went by, and Horace told them a story about one of the farms they passed. A story about the farmer's gambling debts that smacked of gossip.

"I believe I see someone waiting for you, Miss Brady," Horace spoke with an interested enthusiasm over McKenna's head. Irrationally, Una immediately thought Horace was speaking of Henry, but when she looked forward, she saw the large, ruddy figure of Saul standing by the front of the building.

"Yes, thank you." She said when she looked at Saul's impassive face. Almost as soon as she said it, Saul noticed the carriage and its occupants. He stood up straight and moved slowly toward them.

Una hadn't really been sure what she'd thought tonight would be like, but she hadn't expected to spend the whole night by Saul's side. She'd thought he might ask her to dance a few times, but she'd expected to have the freedom to stay with her sister. Leaving McKenna alone with Horace felt like a betrayal. She wasn't ready to be alone with him. She'd barely said a word to him at all, and when she did, Una could hear the panic in her sister's voice.

When Saul walked over to the carriage, Una saw an earnestness that she'd not noticed before. Immediately, she felt bad for the way she felt about him. He didn't look very well put together, but he had made an obvious effort. His hair was brushed back from his face, his clothes were clean and of a good quality, though his shirt looked uncomfortably small to Una. Like he'd done before, he was holding his hat in his hand, and his gaze continually came back to it.

"Hello," Una said when Saul came close enough for him to hear her.

Una watched his mouth move and assumed he was saying the same back to her, though she couldn't actually hear it.

Una waited momentarily, thinking that Saul would give her a hand down from the carriage, but no hand presented itself. Una then started to make her way down on her own. When she turned around, she saw that

McKenna had already been helped down by Horace on the other side of the carriage.

Una looked for her sister, but she couldn't see her on the other side. She walked around but still couldn't find her sister.

"Shall we go in?" Una asked Saul, feeling desperate to find McKenna.

Again he said something so far under his breath that she could not hear him. The sounds of horses clacking into the square and families talking jovially to one another completely overcame Saul's words. Una gave up all hope of hearing him throughout the night.

Una led the way, assuming Saul would follow, which he did. Townspeople turned to look at her as she went. She tried to smile warmly but felt too rushed to find McKenna to do any more than that.

"Did you see where my sister went?" She looked around herself as she moved into the hall with Saul at her heels. He was so tall he must be able to see everything going on in the hall.

Saul said something, and Una's brow crinkled in frustration.

"What?" she said loudly up to him.

"…there…" Was all Una could hear, and she moved closer, tilting her ear upward one more time.

"What was that?"

"Over there by the far door," He said more loudly than Una had ever heard him before. "I think," He added in a self-conscious manner.

Una looked at Saul wide-eyed for a moment before turning to look at the far door that he was talking about. People were streaming into the hall and walking in front of her line of vision. Una walked around a few people before she could make out Horace's head, which meant that McKenna must be there as well.

Una began walking toward Horace's head and finally, when she was closer, the silhouette of her sister became clear. Una walked quickly, moving next to her sister. Saul stood awkwardly beside her, and McKenna turned with a relieved look to Una. Horace was talking to someone Una had never seen before. He was obviously a well-known man that other townspeople wanted to impress. He had a loud, gruff laugh that caught Una off guard the first time she heard it.

"I couldn't find you, and I worried," Una said quietly to her sister.

"Horace sort of… just went off. I had to follow." McKenna looked pained saying it, and Una felt the urge to go home. Saul would surely take them both back if Una asked him to. She could pretend illness or have McKenna pretend illness.

After a good quarter of an hour, a few musicians congregated with their instruments, and Una heard a familiar sweet sound from a fiddle. It wasn't an Irish tune, it wasn't actually anything she'd heard before, but it felt familiar all the same.

Una felt her jaw clench and hot tears fill her eyes. She pinched her hand and forced the emotion that seized her to fall back away. Music held a special power over her that she would never understand.

Una watched as an older couple walked to the middle of the room. The other people standing nearby moved away toward the edge of the room. The couple smiled at one another, then the woman curtseyed as the man gave a small bow. There was an abrupt turn in the music, and the sound began in earnest.

It was a fast tempo, and the couple moved in sync with one another. Soon another couple came out to join them. They were younger, but they were equally skilled in the dance. Third and fourth couples emerged until there was a line of couples dancing in sync most of the way down the room. More people filed in, and Una realized that though Catherine and Joseph may be coming, it was possible that she may not run into them tonight. It was becoming quite crowded, and Una was unsure how anyone could walk around at all.

"Would you like to give it a try?" Horace's voice was loud and travelled to Una's ears though he stood in front of McKenna.

"I don't know," McKenna's eyes turned frightened to the crowd of dancers and her voice was high-pitched.

"You will be fine," Horace said loudly. He held out a hand, and Una looked at the dancers with new eyes. She watched their moves to try and assess whether or not her sister would be fine.

Before she even turned back, McKenna was being led by the hand out to the dance floor. Almost every single person in the new dancing line looked like they were having a good time. Not only were they all having fun, but they were all pretty good dancers. There seemed to be no one else dancing who didn't know what to do. Why hadn't Catherine insisted they learn a few dances before coming?

"We had better go too," Una turned quickly to Saul, who seemed shocked by the notion of dancing at the dance. Una didn't care, she didn't want to leave McKenna out there on her own. At least if they were together then there would be the two of them who didn't know the steps. Una began walking at a fast clip trying to move into the spot just next to McKenna, but before she made it to the line, two other couples had already moved in between McKenna and the end of the line.

Una waited for Saul as another couple moved in, then placed herself next to this couple as Saul arrived. Saul looked almost as scared as McKenna had. Una wasn't at all certain of Saul's abilities or intentions in dancing this evening, and a part of her did feel sorry for the man.

Una looked at the couple next to them and began to try and match her movements with theirs. It was a repeating pattern, and though she looked stilted during the first stanza, she got better through each and found herself at a reasonably competent pace.

Saul, who knew the moves, was not very adept with them, and Una quickly found that her dancing surpassed his. She looked to McKenna, who also looked like she was picking it up, though she didn't look like she was having fun. The girls had spent time learning and doing dances back home. Though these were not the same dances, they had some of the same movements. These particular dances, though fast, were still much slower than what they did at home.

Horace seemed to be having a great time. Each time McKenna came around, he swung her with such force that her feet left the ground. Saul never seemed to make it to Una in time to move her around the way the dance required. So Una just moved herself around and was happy for it.

After another two dances Horace finally decided to leave the floor. Una was happy to have a break and to give Saul a break as well.

"Hello," Catherine was upon Una before she had time to notice her. Horace and McKenna had walked too far off to notice, and Una was afraid to lose them.

"Horace and McKenna are just this way," Una said loudly. She pointed in the direction they'd just gone, but Catherine did not seem compelled to follow them.

"How is it going between them?" Catherine leaned in close to Una as if they were sharing a secret.

Una paused as she watched the look on Catherine's face. Catherine genuinely looked interested and hopeful.

"Okay, I think. I'm not completely sure. I haven't been able to speak with her alone yet."

Catherine didn't look satisfied with Una's answer, but Una just wanted to get past her and on to where McKenna had gone off with Horace.

"I saw you two dancing," Catherine turned her gaze between Una and Saul. Una blushed and looked quickly at Saul who didn't seem to have heard Catherine. "I won't keep you, I can see you're itching to get off to more fun."

Una gave a half-smile as her stomach twisted. Where was Henry anyway? She hadn't seen him yet. Una pushed forward through the crowd in an effort to find McKenna. She looked around every few steps, but the crowd had swallowed her whole. Una looked up to see if she could find an outline of Horace's head, but nothing appeared there either.

"You must be one of the new Irish sisters," said a woman Una had never seen before. When Una looked into her face, she noticed how lovely the woman was. She had dark brown hair and shining brown eyes that were highlighted on her perfect, heart-shaped face.

"Yes, I'm afraid I've not met you," Una said, looking for an introduction.

The woman let out a tinkling laugh that Una could still hear over the din around her.

"I'm so sorry. Of course you have no idea who I am. I'm Cecily Baker, a friend of Henry's. He's told me about you."

Una looked over Cecily Baker's face trying to determine what the other woman meant when she said she was a "friend" of Henry's. What had Henry told her?

"Hello, Saul," Cecily said loudly as she looked up at the older man.

"Hello," Saul spoke loud enough for both Una and Cecily to hear. Una looked at Cecily, but the volume of Saul's voice didn't seem to take her by surprise the way it was taking Una by surprise.

"I'm so sorry, I'm trying to find my sister, if you'll excuse me." Una wanted to ask if Cecily knew where Henry was, but she also didn't want to hear the answer. If Cecily did know, then why didn't Una know as well?

"Of course," Cecily moved out of the way with a smile. "I'm sure we'll meet again very soon."

Una looked over the other woman's face once again to try and comprehend what she meant but found it nearly impossible to see anything past her lovely features and dancing smile.

Una walked forward into the crowd. She brushed past people and could only hope she wasn't being rude. McKenna was nowhere to be found. Una thought she might at least hear Horace's giant laugh, but there was none of that either.

Turning to ask Saul for help in locating her again, she realized that Saul was no longer behind her. She'd lost him somewhere in the shuffle. Una exhaled. She was relieved in part but also worried. She hadn't paid enough attention to him, not the way she should have been.

Suddenly, an overwhelming sense of fatigue overcame her, and Una felt the need of a wall or a chair. She moved slowly to her nearest flanking wall and leaned forward onto it.

"Una," The sound came from her right, and immediately her vision was filled with her sister's face.

"I thought I'd lost you again," Una said as she let her body lean into the wall, trying to smile for her sister.

"Horace is dancing," McKenna said as her eyes looked out to the dance line. Una turned, pressing her back to the wall and looked to the line just as her sister did.

On the dance floor, holding hands with a woman who looked more like a saloon maid than a farmer's wife, was Horace. He was laughing in his booming voice. Una wondered why she hadn't heard him before because it sounded so clear to her now.

"Why is he dancing with another woman? He just left you here on your own?"

"I think they must be old friends. He seems very familiar with her." McKenna looked at them, and Una observed her sister's face. She was too young for this.

~

Una and McKenna kept close to each other for the rest of the night. They saw no sign of Saul or Henry, and Horace danced a few more reels with the woman before disappearing completely. The room was getting hotter as the night wore on, and the punch that was served seemed to sink right into everyone. Una had one glass, but the heat and the alcohol didn't mix well with her. McKenna had two glasses and became positively tipsy.

Una held onto her sister. They occasionally moved around but mostly kept to themselves, saying little and being approached by only two other people all night. One was a man who was so inebriated that he thought Una was his wife, and the other was the infamous pastor who did indeed look red in the face and a bit too bubbly for someone of the clergy.

When the night was over and people were leaving, there was still no sign of Horace. Una became nervous, thinking that he may have left. They would have to walk all the way home in the dark or ask a stranger for a ride.

As the two girls exited the building, there was a large commotion coming from the side of the building.

"That can't be right," one man said.

"It is, and now you'll have to pay up." Una recognized the voice immediately as Horace's. So the man heavily in gambling debt must be a personal acquaintance, with Horace partially to blame for his misfortunes.

Una was exhausted. McKenna was practically asleep on her feet. All both of them could think was that they wanted to go home.

"Mr. Boucher," Una said with an acerbic edge. "Would you be so kind as to see us home?"

"Well," Horace turned to her with surprise, "Miss Brady, it's good of you to remind me."

His voice was sarcastic and playful at the same time, neither of which Una appreciated. It was too late in the evening, and she was just too exhausted to have much patience for any.

"If you go wait in the carriage, I will be right with you."

Una thought of a thousand things she wanted to say, but she bit her tongue and nodded her head instead.

Chapter Ten

Una slept through her earliest work the next morning and awoke with a start as sunlight filled the small bedroom.

McKenna was fast asleep, and the girls were gone.

"McKenna," Una shook her sister. "We've slept in."

Una jumped to her feet and began pulling herself together. Because of Horace, they'd returned home much later than Catherine and Joseph, and by the time they gotten home, the rest of the family was already sound asleep. A sinking sense of panic overtook Una, and she pulled on her clothes as fast as she could.

McKenna took an extra few moments to wake up. She looked at Una without comprehension. She put one fair hand to her forehead and said, "My head hurts." She then realized that they should have been working hours ago.

McKenna fumbled out of bed and to her feet. A peculiar smell clung to both girls from the night before. Una wasn't sure what it was. They had just crept into bed when they got home, both ignoring their need to clean up first.

"We have to clean before going down," Una said as she walked the two short steps to the washbasin. She began a quick clean-up to make herself presentable enough for a day of work. McKenna was pulling on her dress and trying to get her boots out at the same time, which seemed to slow her down rather than speed her up.

McKenna moved to the basin with her boots still unlaced and her hair falling out of place.

As soon as they'd made themselves reasonably presentable, the two girls ran out of the door and down the stairs. No one was in the house, so they continued on to the back.

Catherine was walking back to the house and waved at them with a smile. Una exhaled. She looked happy, not upset at all.

"I'm sorry we slept in, we just got home so late," Una began explaining, then stopped when Catherine didn't seem to care.

"I have some news," Catherine smiled widely. "Horace sent a letter over this morning with one of his boys."

Una's heart quickened, and she stopped moving.

"He's very impressed with McKenna," Catherine said as she looked from one girl to the other. "He likes you. He thinks you will make a nice match, and he would like to continue moving forward with your arrangements. You must have done something right last night."

"Oh," Una said as Catherine's news began to sink in.

"Is that all you have to say? This is great news. He is the wealthiest man in town, maybe for three towns over. He's handsome and will certainly settle a nice sum on you." Catherine looked from one to the other again. She said, "He will pay off all of your expenses since you've both come to me." Catherine stared at them both, then made a surprised sound, "I thought you would both be pleased."

Una looked to McKenna, who had gone white. She turned back to Catherine, "We are. It's just…"

"Just what?" Catherine's voice began to harden.

"It's just that we barely know him. I think there may be some questions about his—" Una looked for the right word but nothing was overly forthcoming. "About his character."

Catherine's face immediately changed.

"Questions about his character? You would do well to keep that notion to yourself. And what of your expenses? Do you think those just disappear when you're both married and out of the house?"

"Well…" Una began.

"Well what?" Catherine's voice was high and tight, and Una could tell that she was treading on thin ice.

"It's just, I thought that with our help—in the fields and with the animals—that we would be making up most of our expenses?"

Catherine bristled, and Una felt a coldness clamp down on her stomach.

"I believe there is some work in the field that could use your attention now. You are both a little late this morning, aren't you?"

Una felt a cold grip on her heart. She'd never seen this side of Catherine before. "Yes, ma'am—I'll just—" Una walked off toward the field she was going to work in today. Catherine made an additional comment to McKenna quietly so that Una couldn't hear. Una had the impulse to stop and try to listen anyway but decided that she'd had enough to do with Catherine for one day.

The morning went by quickly. Una skipped lunch to continue her work since she'd missed the early morning hours.

When she came in for dinner, she decided that she should try to stay on Catherine's good side. If she was going to have any pull with her about Horace, then maybe she should try to keep things good between them.

"Did you have a good day?" Una asked before heading upstairs to wash and change for dinner.

"Mmm," Catherine hummed noncommittally but said nothing.

Una nodded and looked at the ceiling trying to think of what she should do. Ultimately, nothing came to her, so she went upstairs and took her time getting ready for dinner before coming down and taking her seat.

"I've moved you over here," Catherine said, indicating a chair that would put two of the children between her and McKenna. "If you don't mind, I think McKenna would be a good influence on Martha."

Catherine looked at Una icily until Una stood and moved over two seats. What Catherine really meant was that she thought Una was being a bad influence on her own sister. The children came in, and Catherine indicated the newly appointed chairs. Una watched McKenna sit down and felt that Catherine's actions were meant to directly hurt her.

Una stayed quiet for most of dinner until Joseph started talking about the night before.

"Catherine," Una looked to the other woman and waited for her aunt to turn her face to her. "Do you know someone named Cecily Baker?"

"Yes, she's Henry's fiancé," Catherine snapped, looking back at Una. Una's insides turned upside down.

Joseph spoke up. "They're not engaged, are they? Not formally?"

"Well, maybe not formally, I don't know." Catherine turned from her husband back to Una. "But everyone in town knows that they are intended for one another."

Joseph shrugged and took another bite of the seconds Catherine had pulled for him.

"They've been in love since they were children. Everyone knows that," Catherine said in a matter-of-fact tone as she began to pick up the dishes from the children.

Una stood to help.

"I'm fine," Catherine said when she saw Una carrying things over from the table. "Having you help me won't make our meal any less expensive."

Una felt like dropping her plates and slapping Catherine across the face. Didn't she know where they'd come from? Did she really have no heart in her at all? It didn't matter. Una didn't care. Part of her wanted to sleep in and pull back on her duties since they weren't helping anyway, and the other half wanted to wake up earlier, get more done, and prove Catherine wrong.

"Did you see Henry last night?" Catherine said as Una turned.

"No," Una turned back, uncertain where Catherine was headed.

"Well, since you're talking about Cecily, I figured that you must have seen her. So, naturally I thought you would have seen Henry too. They were together all night. He danced with her exclusively, which was funny since I remember him saying he was going to teach you some of the dances."

Una looked to the floor, trying to keep herself under control. Her body was bursting for a fight with this woman. Her own relative. Her own blood.

"I guess that's just the way young men are," Catherine turned to hold Una's eyes. "One minute they promise something, and the next minute they forget all about it."

Una opened her mouth ready to defend Henry.

"Perhaps," was all Una could manage.

Chapter Eleven

Days passed without another word from Horace, Saul, or Henry. Una's defiant side won out, and she found herself waking up long before anyone else did to get more work done. Even Joseph couldn't manage that much in one day. Her fingers bled, her feet grew numb, and she skipped lunch and went back to finish putting her things away after dinner.

Una began to go right to bed after dinner so she would be able to do it all again the next day.

McKenna became silent and withdrawn, and Una understood all too well what she was unhappy about.

There had to be a way to have more control over their fate. Una could see now that Catherine would not be helping them anymore. She would do no more for the girls than she already had, and she expected their marriages to happen soon. Catherine stopped speaking to Una entirely unless it was to tell her about some work that needed to be done.

After four days of heavy, strained tension, Una looked up from putting her tools away to see Henry. The sun was almost gone, so she had to squint to make sure she was really seeing him and not a shadow that looked like him. Una stopped her movements.

Henry said nothing. Una wondered how long he'd been standing there in the oncoming darkness. She turned and looked toward the house, then walked further over toward the barn so that there was no chance that she could be observed from inside.

"You shouldn't be here," Una said in a husky whisper.

Henry shifted his weight. "I didn't see you at the dance," He seemed cautious to Una.

"I was there, your brother must have told you. He found me right away." Una pressed her hands into her dress while taking in a shaky breath. "I've been going to sleep early so I can get extra work done. I should probably…" She pointed toward the house.

"Yes, of course."

"Was there something you came to tell me?" Una's voice was harder than it needed to be, but she was trying to make up for all the soft thoughts and tempting dreams that blossomed in his presence. She braced as she tried to prepare herself for news of Cecily, preparing for the true clarification of reality.

"You talked to Cecily, right? She told me that she introduced herself," he said. His words sounded different than they normally did. Everything about him felt different now that she understood what reality was.

"Don't worry, I give you my blessing," Una snapped as she began to walk toward the house. Henry stepped forward, grabbing her wrist and pulling her to the wall before she could go any further.

"It's not what you think," he whispered, his face close to hers. She tried not to look at the miniature pieces that made up his face. She didn't want to remember this the way she remembered their kiss that day by the tree.

"What do I think?" Una asked.

"I'm not engaged to her. I'm not romantic with her. We've been friends since childhood, and there have always been rumors, but that's it."

Una felt her heart beating heavily in her chest.

"It doesn't matter what I think, Henry." Una pulled her arm free from his grip. She walked forward four feet, then swung around and returned. "We have both been—we've been made ridiculous. Catherine can tell how I feel about you. I'm sure of it now. She's… I can't stay here any longer. I have to be okay moving forward, and you should be too."

"What do you mean?"

"I mean just that. I have to get married, Henry. Catherine is growing tired of having us here, and we need to leave. I have to help McKenna some way, and I don't know how, but I can't do anything while I live here. You aren't free…"

Henry opened his mouth as if about to speak.

"No, please. You are not free, and you can't say that you are. Your brother…" Una watched Henry's face as she spoke, "what about your brother?" Una rubbed her lips together and looked off into the field. "It's okay, we will both be fine, just not together." Una turned and walked quickly toward the house. She waited for the sound of his voice to stop her.

She could imagine the touch of his hand, but nothing reached out to her. Her fingers reached for the door, and still there was nothing from Henry. Una paused as if she'd just not heard, as if there were something more to come, and she had just to wait. But nothing came. Henry did not stop her, and Una went inside.

Chapter Twelve

The sight of Horace in his carriage with the same pompous look on his face set Una reeling. She and McKenna watched him jump down from his carriage and walk into the house. There was the sound of his loud footfalls and his belly laugh, though Una couldn't figure out what he could be laughing about with Catherine. To her mind, Catherine was not a humorous woman.

Una and McKenna took up seats on the floor next to the bedroom door. Una cracked the door so that the sound of Catherine, Joseph, and Horace came floating up easily.

Catherine had told both girls first thing in the morning that Horace was anxious to make his marriage to McKenna simple and soon. He needed help with the children, and McKenna was the perfect solution. He needed a wife, had needed one for the past year, and he didn't feel like waiting any longer than he had to.

McKenna had shrunk at the sound of this, and Catherine had turned her cold eyes on Una.

"Can I be here for the conversation? She is my younger sister."

"No," Catherine said as she pulled out a folded piece of creamy paper. "He says specifically that he would like to talk to Joseph and me, nothing about you."

"Maybe you could ask when he comes?"

Catherine looked at Una with a tilt of her head and said, "Yes, of course."

Una was listening for the question and was waiting to make her way down the stairs and into the meeting. She couldn't bear the thought of things going on without her input. She needed to ask Horace some questions, to push the wedding as far ahead as possible.

Catherine began talking to Horace, but there was no mention of Una joining the conversation. Catherine did not mention Una at all.

"You have made a wonderful choice," Catherine gushed, and Una could practically hear the dollar signs in her eyes. Were the Donnellys really so very poor that they needed to scrape up whatever Horace Boucher was willing to leave them? It didn't feel that way to Una, but she also didn't understand Catherine's actions for any other reason. She could see as well as Una could that McKenna was not interested in marrying this man. There could be very little question.

Behind the fear of McKenna's marriage to such a man, Una forgot almost completely about her own plight. Her own happiness seemed like nothing compared to the happiness of her younger sister. McKenna was her only living sibling and practically her only living relative. Una had begun to consider Catherine as less than family. She didn't know how she would classify her, but to Una, family was loving, family was something much more than what Catherine had become.

"When is the soonest we can arrange this?" Horace's voice lifted easily up the stairs and to the expectant ears of both sisters. Una put her arm around her sister as they listened. Her love for McKenna overwhelmed her, and Una had to force herself to listen. She could not barge in. She could not make her presence known or insert herself in the conversation even though she wanted to.

"As soon as you'd like. What are you thinking?"

"I was thinking two weeks? Is that enough time to get her ready? I'll leave some money here so you can arrange for her to have some material or some dresses made. She can't wear what she's been wearing when she comes under my roof. I want at least one new dress and three in the process of being made when she moves to the farm." Horace sounded comfortable giving off his demands. He made it so easy for Una to imagine him hovering over his new wife, punishing her when she was unable to follow his directions perfectly. "And I'm not interested in her older sister visiting. I don't like being told what to do by a woman. Something tells me that the older one is quite adept at giving her opinion wherever she sees fit."

"That shouldn't be a problem," Catherine said quickly. Joseph was saying very little, just an agreeing hum every now and again. Una was certain that she could hear a smile in Catherine's voice as she so easily exiled Una from seeing her sister ever again.

Una held McKenna closer. She craved McKenna's presence, but she also needed McKenna to anchor her to the floor, to keep her from running downstairs and yelling at each person as if they'd said nothing of great importance at all.

"I don't want to go with him. I can't," McKenna whispered to Una.

Una let her hand trace over her sister's hair and said, "I know."

Had they come so far together only to be split up now? Were they to slowly become strangers living in the same town?

"We will figure it out, somehow," Una whispered back as the crack of Horace's voice came bounding up the stairs to them.

"I will go make the arrangements at the church then," Horace's voice became even clearer, and Una could tell that he was standing. So that was it. They'd sat together for ten minutes deciding the fate of a fragile sixteen-year-old girl. Was that really all the time they could give her?

Good. Leave, Una thought. *Go away and never come back.*

They listened to Horace talk to Joseph as they left the house. There was the sound of their voices coming from the front of the house for a minute or two, another loud laugh, then the sound of Horace mounting the carriage and driving off. There was no sound of the front door opening again, so Joseph must have gone back to work around the back of the house.

Una had to talk to Catherine.

Catherine's shoes could be heard clacking on the wood floors as she walked around.

Una swallowed a lump in her throat and tried to make herself as open and relatable as possible. Catherine couldn't be completely insensitive to what Una was feeling now, could she be? It seemed impossible for Catherine not to understand what Una was going through or for the older woman to want pain and suffering to come to her own kin.

Una walked quietly down the steps and watched the other woman as she moved across the room.

"Catherine?" Una steadied her voice as she stood erect on the last step. Catherine turned to look at her, and Una took the final step down. She stood level with Catherine now, who had stopped picking up to look at Una.

"You heard everything then?" She flicked her eyes toward the ceiling.

"Yes, of course." Una had the urge to tell her that she'd heard that Catherine hadn't asked about Una being a part of the conversation, but she hadn't walked down here for that. There were other, more important, things to think of now. "McKenna is my sister. I love her as much as you love your daughters."

Catherine exhaled through her nose, "And what is it that you're upset about now?"

"I think you know," Una took a gulp of air and pressed her fingernails into her hands to keep herself steady and strong. "I can't let McKenna marry that man. I won't be kept from my sister. Our entire family died, and she's all I have. She needs me as much as I need her."

Catherine readjusted herself and raised her voice, saying, "There is a difference, a very large difference between a sister and a daughter. You don't know this yet because you don't have children. But you will know it soon." Catherine looked out of one of the back windows for a glimpse of her children. "You will both have a new family now. When you both have your first child, you will forget about this bond you have. You will have your children to look after, a new family to care about."

"That's not true. I will always love my sister. I will always care about her. Did you have brothers and sisters?" Una asked as she felt the air in the room compress around her body.

"Yes, and I had to leave them just like everyone else does. I haven't seen my brothers or sisters in years. My parents were poor immigrants from Ireland just like you and your sister. They did what they had to do to survive, and you will too."

"No," Una's voice came out in a sharp bark, and Catherine blanched at the sound of it. "I'm sorry, but I will not lose my sister." There was so much Una wanted to say but not enough words to say it with. Una made the walk over to the window Catherine had just looked out of. Catherine followed her, and they both watched little Joe run after a goat while the girls were in the process of making something together. Perhaps it was a new piece of the hutch for the chickens.

"Why did you choose McKenna for Horace?" Una's voice softened as she watched the children. "Why didn't you choose me? I'm older, I would have been stronger to move in with three children and a widower who …" she motioned into the air at some word she could not find.

"I didn't choose McKenna. He asked for McKenna. Horace wanted McKenna because she is young. Sixteen is a good age, an age where one can work hard, bear children, and still be molded into the woman that he wants her to be. You are a perfect example of a woman already firmly molded into your preconceived notions and habits. You would have made his life terrible, can you deny that?"

"Do you care more about his wellbeing than your own kin? Don't you care at all what is best for us?"

"Haven't I showed that already? I paid for you to come from Boston all the way out here. I didn't have that sort of money. I paid for your dresses, for your food. It is my responsibility to get you on to your own lives. I helped put meat back on your bones. There is no more I can do for you. I can't keep you here. It's time for you both to go, and I don't want to discuss it anymore."

Una opened her mouth trying to think of something to say in reply. Something that would move Catherine and change her mind, but there was nothing. Catherine's face had hardened, and she wasn't going to be moved. There was no step forward to take, nothing else to be done. Una looked up toward the floor where her sister sat at that very moment, listening to everything they said.

"Please," Una said, turning to Catherine. "Just think about it. Just take a day or two and think about it."

"Una," Catherine's voice relented into a slightly pitying tone. "I know you think I'm terrible. That I'm heartless and mean, but I'm not. I know what is best for you. I know what the world is like, and I am making sure you and McKenna have a spot in it. There is nothing for me to think about. I'm sorry, I really am. But, maybe you could just embrace this? You know that McKenna will never be okay with Horace if you are not okay with their marriage. You are the only person who can help her prepare for her very real future." Catherine paused. "Are you going to help your sister, or are you going to make this harder for her?"

Una looked out the window again. Little Joe ran straight into Sarah, knocking her to the ground. "If they had a chance to stay together, to help each other and love each other for the rest of their lives, wouldn't you want that for them?"

Catherine sighed with a weariness Una could relate to. "What I want and what is real and possible are two different things."

Chapter Thirteen

True to her word, Catherine did not appear to think about Una's plea. Nor did she mention anything about it to her after their conversation. Two days later when Horace had a chance to go to the church, he sent word that they would have to wait an additional week because the pastor was going to be visiting family. This meant that a visiting pastor would be holding the local parish until he was back. They would wait for their own pastor.

The glitch gave the Brady girls an extra week but no extra promise.

They went into town for material for the first time since they'd purchased their original dress material. The money Horace had given for the dresses had not been inconsequential. Una made suggestions about each fabric, and she smiled when McKenna lost herself in the feel of something particularly fine. Their situation seemed desperate, but Una held tightly to the little bit of hope that she could.

Material was purchased. A soft pink, white linen, mustard-colored muslin, and a plain gray that Una thought was good for McKenna's plainer days.

Catherine released McKenna from any further work and set her to cutting and sewing the dresses that would go with her to Horace's farm when they married. Catherine also had McKenna soak her hands and callouses every night. McKenna was to brush her hair one hundred times a night with extra care and put in plaits carefully done before bed. McKenna was in a preparing stage from Catherine. Una tried to keep her mind positive, though the evidence of the future was not looking particularly bright.

As the days wore on and the promise of an upcoming marriage seemed to only increase with time, Una began to stay awake at night. Her brain tried in vain to create a solution. There was no good way out, Una concluded. Everything was difficult. She didn't care is she upset Catherine anymore, but where would they go and what would they do if they were to run away?

It would be different if Horace were a good man in Una's estimation, but he wasn't. Una felt instinctively that he was would be a hard and mean husband. A man with other women and gambling on the side. It was no way for any woman to live, let alone her baby sister. Their parents had displayed a loving relationship between them. Their father never forced his will on their mother. There was laughter in their house. There was a love that spread out around them and wrapped them each up.

Because of their family, money had never seemed like the most important issue to Una. Now that her entire family had died from a lack of it, her perspective had changed, but not enough to include Horace. Una could now see the value in security; the value of a man who could see you through the hardest of times. It must be the hardest thing in the world to see your children die because there was not enough money to save them.

But there was still the question of love. Respect. Happiness. What of those things? Hadn't they lost enough? Why live a bad life when there was potential to live a good one right next to it?

Una decided that if it came to it, then they would just leave in the middle of night. They could be farm hands as they went or dairymaids or something. Anything would be better than to be separated from each other forever.

The days wore on, and Una began to feel her sleepless nights. The exhausting days begin to drain her energy. Her body was tired, she'd begun to lose weight all over again. Una caught glances from Catherine, but she no longer cared how she appeared to the other woman. Pieces of her were falling away, and it was all she could do to function each day.

"We are taking off from our normal work today," Catherine said one morning as Una was about to head out to the fields.

Una hesitated. "Why is that?" she asked suspiciously. She wouldn't put it past Catherine to lie about the wedding date so that Una didn't have a proper chance of escaping with her sister. Una was sure, however, that Catherine would never suspect her of being capable of running away with no proper prospects or food while they each had the potential for a life of security.

"There is a picnic auction tonight. You each make a basket, and your beau bids on it. There is usually a bit of competition among the men, but I am certain that both Saul and Horace will come out as the winners for both you girls." Catherine made a face indicating that Una and McKenna ought to be excited about this. Neither girl rose to the bait. It would not be fun for either one. It would be harder work than their normal daily routine.

"Oh," Una looked at the baskets that were set out. She hadn't noticed them before. "When is the auction?"

"Tonight." Catherine had begun to look down to her work, and she didn't look up as she answered this.

"Why didn't you tell us sooner?" Una couldn't even manage a half-smile for Catherine.

"Didn't I?" Catherine looked up with an overly innocent look. "I'm sorry, I thought I did. Well, no harm done. There is plenty of time for you both to fill your baskets."

Una nodded and looked at McKenna, who was eating the last of her breakfast bread.

"I meant to tell you," Catherine looked to Una. "Saul has mentioned an interest in setting a date," Catherine said this as her eyes turned back to the vegetables she was chopping.

"Did he?"

"I think tonight could be a good time to set one. Don't you?"

Una pulled her eyebrows together looking at Catherine. She waited for Catherine's appraising look to find her before saying, "I don't know."

"Don't be silly. It's been long enough. McKenna will be gone soon, and you don't want to be the old maid of the family, waiting around for her beau for the next few years. I imagine that would be somewhat embarrassing for you."

"I don't think so," Una shook her head. "I don't suppose I feel those sorts of rules are much of anything to be heeded, the ones about older and younger siblings."

A muscle in Catherine's forehead moved. Spending the next few hours in the kitchen with Catherine was a terrible thought for Una. Every word Catherine said felt like an insult. Una had to bite her lip and constantly try to clear her head as the day went on.

The young girls were with the animals. McKenna did as she was told. Una didn't feel like she could talk to her sister while Catherine was around, so the small group worked mostly in silence for the day. Just before lunch, Catherine went out to check on the girls and little Joe.

Una looked at the pies that were in the process of being made. Three entire pies for each basket. No wonder Catherine thought the girls cost so much money, Catherine was throwing all her money into getting each of them married off to someone who could pay her back many fold for her money and efforts.

"McKenna, would you mind running upstairs to check on our green dresses for tonight?"

"Didn't you do that earlier?"

Una looked at her sister, "Yes, but I think I missed something. Would you mind double-checking? I'll watch over your food."

McKenna nodded and turned to go upstairs. With Catherine in the barn and McKenna upstairs, Una took out the salt. She lifted a heaping scoop and put it down into the pie crust, then quickly added the filling contents so that the evidence was completely obscured. Una took another heaping scoop and did the same to her own pie. She made sure her filling was on right away, so that if either her sister or Catherine walked in, neither would know what she was up to.

Una turned and looked around her to make sure Catherine hadn't come back yet. There was no perfect way to tell that each pie went with the right person, so the only sure thing to do would be…another large scoop of salt into Catherine's crust. She plopped the filling down, and when all the evidence was removed, she replaced the salt bag to its original spot.

"Everything looks fine on our dresses," McKenna said as she walked down the stairs. McKenna was making her first two dresses at the same time, and so far neither was done.

"Good," Una looked up casually at her sister. "I don't know why I thought I missed something. Thank you for checking." Una picked up her own pie, "Shall we?"

"Ready to bake?"

Una nodded, and the girls loaded all of their three pies in their baskets.

By dinnertime, the girls were exhausted, and there was no food but day-old bread and cheese for dinner. Everyone ate sparingly before Una and McKenna were sent upstairs to change for the evening.

Una hadn't asked who was picking them up, who was taking them, or any pertinent details about the evening. She was desperate to know the answers to many different questions, but each would require a conversation with Catherine, and that was out of question.

Una watched her sister dress carefully. When she watched her like this, McKenna seemed much younger than her sixteen years. She was still small for her age from her malnutrition, but she'd also begun to grow as soon as she'd had some proper food in her system. Her body was filling out, but she still had a young way of moving, of looking at the world around her, of humming when she thought no one noticed—perhaps when even she herself didn't notice. These things seemed to make her young, much younger than sixteen.

Both Brady girls were in their green dresses, but this time Una kept both of their hairstyles simple, no flowers, nothing fancy. In fact, everything was rather plain. They looked respectable, but nothing more, just the way Una wanted it.

Catherine said nothing about this when they were called downstairs. Una had been prepared for Catherine to be up in arms. She could imagine Catherine sending them back upstairs to look more like a romantic figure than a schoolmarm.

The little girls had found their way inside and little Joe was on Catherine's lap. The Brady girls took seats as they waited for further news of their journey, but Catherine said nothing. It was a good while of sitting before a noise caught Una's attention.

To Una's dismay, she heard the wheels of a carriage or wagon and the hoof beats of horses outside of the house.

"Ah," Catherine looked up. "I believe we have one of your escorts."

Una's heart sank again. They were being split up this time.

A knock rang out, and Catherine opened the door as both girls got to their feet. Horace was on the other side, and he looked just as he did for the dance.

"Good evening," Horace grinned at McKenna. He looked down at the basket she was holding. "Is that for me?"

"Now you'll just have to wait until the auction like every other man," Catherine seemed more pleased with Horace than anyone else in the house.

"I can't make any promises, but I'll do my best," Horace took the basket, then held the door for McKenna. "After you," he said. McKenna gave a quick fleeting glance to Una, then walked out in front of Horace.

Catherine walked out onto the porch as the two got into the carriage, then she waved as they drove off. There was no Little Joe running after the carriage this time. Una sat back down and wondered when Saul would show.

There was a new rattle, and Una sat up a bit straighter. At least she would be out of this house and away from Catherine. Perhaps they could even move fast enough to catch up to the other carriage.

For the second time, there was a knock at the door. Catherine opened it with gusto, and on the other side stood…Henry.

"Henry," Catherine's voice dropped as she saw him.

"I'm here for Una. Saul had to go to town for business today, so I volunteered to take Una there this evening."

Una's heart leaped wildly as she watched Henry's face and his mouth move. She didn't trust herself with this man. She didn't trust herself in the least.

"Your brother will be in attendance tonight, I hope," Catherine's voice sounded worried.

"Of course," Henry smiled and threw the question off. He turned and looked at Una. "Are you ready, my lady?"

Una nodded as her cheeks lit up. Surely if Catherine didn't already know, then she would know soon. Una's face and coloring was bound to give her true feelings away if nothing else did.

"Be sure this stays safe during the ride. It is for Saul," Catherine said pointedly about the basket.

"Of course," Una said with a bright levity she hadn't felt in days, something she shouldn't be feeling at all.

Chapter Fourteen

The two sat in silence as Henry's wagon pulled away from the house and into the road.

"I have been thinking about you since I came here the other day," Henry's voice, breaking the silence, was soft but urgent. It was a different sound than it had been only a few minutes before in the entrance to the Donnelly house. He had sounded young and light then, but now she could hear the weight he was really carrying around.

"Yes?" Una tried not to voice the excitement that had been bubbling in her since she'd seen Henry and not Saul at the door.

Henry said nothing in response and rode forward in silence for the next ten minutes.

"Is Saul really in town today?" Una asked. She'd been hoping Henry would just provide the information, but the silence was dragging on her nerves.

"Yes," Henry looked at her quickly, then turned his eyes back to the road.

Una nodded. It was not the answer that she had wanted to hear. She'd wanted to think that Henry had contrived to pick her up somehow, not that he'd really just filled in at the last minute to pick her up.

"Will you be buying Cecily's basket?" Una asked as her face grew red once again.

Henry shifted awkwardly in his seat, "I was thinking I might."

"Oh," Una watched the bob of the horse's head and the swish of its mane.

"But, I was also thinking that I might bid on yours."

"Mine?" Una turned back to Henry. "But your brother? What about Saul?"

"Yes, my brother. I don't suppose I thought it all the way through. It just seemed like a good idea when I was alone doing my work. I thought—maybe if I could just show people how I felt… maybe Saul would realize, maybe he would just…"

"No, I don't think he would just… I think he wouldn't understand, or perhaps wouldn't believe it at all." Una pulled the pieces together in her mind but found herself unable to say more about Saul. "We just found out about the picnic today. Catherine didn't tell us, probably because she thinks I'm going to sabotage her plans for marrying us off."

"Are you?" Henry smiled at the thought. "Going to sabotage her plans, I mean?"

"That's my plan, though I don't know how. So far my only solution is running away."

"No, you can't do that," Henry said quickly, his voice so sincere that Una looked at him, startled.

"Can't I?" Una watched Henry, wondering what his plan was. How could he say that and then let Una marry his brother? It was all so complicated and messy.

Henry didn't appear to have the answers that Una craved, so she turned her focus back to the horses. Her body felt the jolt they made with each step. She let the rock and sway of the wagon take up the better part of her mental processes.

"I envy horses," she said as she watched the manes swish again. "They work hard, but they are also able to run. They can move freely, uninhibited, faster than almost anything else."

Una felt Henry's eyes on her. She looked out over the field to her right. She was suddenly embarrassed by her own words, her reckless exclamation.

"I can understand that," Henry's eyes pulled away from Una, and she was able to focus back on the horses in front of her. "But I don't suppose we have a choice. This is what we've been given, though being a horse might be much more satisfying." He said it in a funny way that made Una laugh. She hadn't laughed in days, and it felt wonderful. It loosened her face, and even her body felt lighter as the laughter seeped out of her.

"What would happen tonight if you did bid on my basket?"

"Probably nothing in the beginning. Then, as the bids got higher, the town would begin to talk. I would go over my brother's best bid to be the winner and then... I don't know. People gossip. People would wonder and assume they knew exactly what was going on. That's what they do in small towns. Everyone figures everything out, then they share it around whether it's true or not."

"That's no good," Una's voice was exhaled out on a whisper.

"No, I don't suppose it is."

"You can't bid. It's no good. You can't let your brother be the center of gossip. I wouldn't want that for him."

Henry nodded but didn't say anything to her in response.

"What about Horace, is there anything else about him that I should know? Anything you didn't say at dinner the night you came?"

"I don't know. He's very highly esteemed here. He never seems to be on the wrong side of anyone, though he does his share of mischief."

"What kind of mischief?"

Henry didn't answer but narrowed his eyes as if trying to find the right words.

"Does it have something to do with the woman he was dancing with at the hall? Or maybe gambling?"

Henry looked over and nodded a little bit. "Yes. You could say both of those things. I don't really know what is true and what isn't true, but there are certain things that make the gossip seem just a little more true."

Una wanted to explain about McKenna, wanted Henry's advice, but they were almost there, and Una felt her throat tighten. The last thing she needed was another night of "fun" ruined by her emotions.

When they arrived at the hall, Una began to have bad memories of the dance. It was only two weeks ago that she'd come here in Horace's carriage. The long night she'd spent mostly standing against the wall. The crowds of people. Horace playing cards, Horace dancing with that other woman. The pastor drinking the punch.

"I don't feel like being here tonight. I don't suppose I would under normal circumstances," Una said.

"I'm just happy that I get to see you," Henry spoke low and under his voice, yet Una could understand every word of his in a way that she never could with Saul.

Una looked at him. His eyes met hers, and she felt like she may never be able to look away again. There was more in his eyes tonight than she'd seen before. He was clear and open, but his heavy energy betrayed him.

Dragging her eyes away, she looked toward the building. Standing just as he had been for the dance, was Saul. His hands were in his pockets this time, and he stood with his hat still on his head.

"Your brother," Una said to Henry.

"Yes, my brother."

~

"Will you talk to me again?" Henry gripped onto her arm just before she began her decent to the ground.

"What about your brother?" She did not look Henry in the eye this time.

"Please." Henry's voice was full of emotion, and Una could not crush that sound.

"Of course," she said just before she went to the ground where Saul was waiting. Henry disappeared almost immediately. Una was left with Saul. She tried out a few questions, though she was never completely sure what Saul was saying in return, so it didn't do much in the way of communication.

In some ways Una was becoming glad that Saul barely spoke to her. The fact that his speech was inaudible and that they spent most of their time in near silence didn't seem to be such a bad thing anymore. With her mind being so active for days on end, a good silence felt like a luxury she couldn't normally afford.

"I think my sister came already," Una said, looking toward the front door. "Shall we go look for them?"

Saul didn't really nod, but a guttural mutter seemed to close the issue. Una turned and walked into the hall. Her basket was in hand, and she looked around before walking over to the space where baskets seemed to be lined up together.

"You can set it here, then when the auction begins, you will need to pick up your basket and hold onto it until you are called up." Cecily had appeared out of nowhere. She was now whispering in Una's ear as she looked at the information spread out in front of her.

Una turned to the other woman. She recognized her voice immediately. The sight of her face brought back the feelings she'd had the first time Una had met her, a feeling very close to jealousy.

"Hello," Una tried to sound as friendly as possible. "You did say you would be seeing me soon, and I guess you were right."

"See, I have insight about these things. That, and I knew this auction was coming soon."

Una asked, "Do you know where the money for the baskets goes?"

Cecily looked at the baskets in front of her. "This year it all goes to the church. It's a new building, and it still needs new Bibles and other things that one assumes all churches should have."

"That's nice," Una looked to where Cecily's eyes were attracted. She looked over the baskets. Some were very big and some very small. "What's in all of these?"

"Same things as yours, I'm sure. Some meats, savory pies, sweet pie, various other treats depending on the woman creating the basket." Cecily turned to look behind herself. She pointed to a small wisp of a woman. "That woman is married to that basket," Cecily said, pointing out a large basket in the front. Una could see treats lifting the lid. It was monstrous and obviously packed to the top. There had to be twice or three times as much in that basket than in her own.

"She is famous for her baskets. They tend to get bids from everyone." Cecily looked over the others. Una didn't know if Cecily was trying to find extra baskets to dissect, or if she was just looking over the goods in general.

"Which one is yours?" Una asked. She looked over the baskets and tried to guess which basket could be lovely enough to match this woman.

"None of them. I almost never do a basket myself. Mostly I just bid on the baskets that no one else is going to buy, then I have a huge feast the next day."

Una laughed. "That sounds like a wonderful idea, if you can afford it."

"Men would demand their money back if they tasted my cooking, so I am really doing them a favor." Cecily looked over the baskets again. "See," she pointed, "I think that one might go unpurchased. I will probably buy it, and the basket itself will end up being deceptively large on the inside."

"I should go," Una said turning to look for Saul.

"Don't worry, he's right there," Cecily pointed to a corner where Saul was sitting.

"Thank you," Una turned to go, then turned back around. "Good luck getting a good basket this year. I suggest you don't pick mine, even if I get zero bids."

"I know two men who are already prepared to buy you out, so I wouldn't worry too much, if I were you."

Una nodded and turned back to Saul. *Two men*, Cecily had said. She was a friend of Henry's. Una let the edges of her mouth curl up as she gently took a seat next to Saul.

Una didn't see McKenna anywhere for a long time. She walked around the perimeter of the hall, then around the outside of the building. The sun had gone down, and Una looked into the darkness for her sister but saw nothing.

By the time she made it back into the building, it was almost full. Una felt the same terrible sensation she'd felt two weeks before but willed herself to look around as she walked.

She found her way back to Saul but found no sign of McKenna as she went. There was a small speech given by the pastor. He talked about the value of Bibles and of pews in the church, then went on to give examples in the Bible of how people gave up their money in tithing only to receive it back tenfold.

As the first basket went up for auction, Una felt unreasonably nervous. She'd picked up her basket and would be called up at some point. Her hands were sweaty. The thought of standing in front of a crowd of people was so incredibly unappealing to her that she briefly considered taking to her heels and running away. Once again, she imagined Saul taking her home early. She was sure she could persuade him to.

As the next person went and the next, the noise level in the room rose. There were hoots from the men. Small groups of people would burst out into laughter or applause at random moments. Una went to get herself a glass of punch since she still had a while to wait before they got to her, and she was feeling the need to calm her nerves.

"Hi," Henry was standing next to her, and there was something of the old sparkle in his eyes.

"Want a cup?" Una gestured to the punch, and Henry picked one up for himself and drank it down in one long sip.

"Your basket is coming up soon, isn't it?"

"There are a few more to go, I think—"

There was another burst of applause as the highest bidder was called and the basket was won. The winner walked up to the stage and took the basket from the woman who seemed just as embarrassed as Una already felt.

"…Next on our list is the new little Irish beauty, McKenna Brady." The announcer's voice rang through the room and fell with a clang on Una's ears. Una turned to the stage. She'd not been able to find her sister once during the evening, yet there was McKenna stepping onto the small platform. Her body looked stiff, and her eyes kept falling to the floor. The basket, which was puny by the standards of some of the women, looked large in her little arms.

"Henry," Una said, turning to him, "would you do something for me?"

"Now, let's give this little lass a true American welcome tonight." The announcer's words elicited a few rough cheers from men in the crowd.

"Of course. What?" Henry's face immediately became serious at the sound of her tone.

Una looked back to McKenna's pale face, and asked Henry, "Will you bid on her basket?"

"I know of at least one man ready to make a good settlement for the... contents... of this remarkable-looking basket." The auctioneer looked at Horace, who crossed his arms and smiled as he walked his feet out into a wider stance.

"She will get bids, I'm sure of it," Henry looked up at McKenna. His point seemed proved as one hand went up, then another. A man called out from the side of the room and another from the back. Una looked around herself in surprise. Many men were bidding. She looked up to McKenna whose eyes were off of the floor and flying from man to man with a look of terror. It was not what she expected.

Horace's voice boomed loudly into the hall, giving a good show in the front of the room. He bid on her basket loudly, letting the whole room know that McKenna Brady belonged to him now.

"Please, will you bid? I can't let Horace win." Una's face crumpled in frustration. The desperation in her voice was so intense that Henry must have understood just how serious Una was about it.

Henry turned toward the stage. "I'll—um, three dollars," Henry called from where he stood.

The bidding continued, and people seemed fascinated that the numbers continued to climb.

"Six dollars," Henry called again with more confidence.

Una was beginning to feel the folly of her ways. Henry would never be able to outbid Horace, not if he was really so much richer than Henry. She looked to her sister, and a sour sickness welled in her stomach. McKenna looked so young, her eyes so wide. She looked more like she was standing trial with a possible execution at the end.

Horace kept his joviality going and gave a laugh here and there. Slowly all the other bidders dropped out until it was just Henry and Horace left.

"Eight twenty-five," Henry said.

Una moved forward as she looked between her sister and Henry. "I'm sorry. I shouldn't have asked you—"

"Eleven dollars," Henry said in response to Horace's next number. Una felt relief overwhelm her for the moment, followed by immediate guilt for Henry. If only she had her own money.

"Please, you have to stop now. I can never repay you for this. It's too much."

"Thirteen," Horace jumped again. The crowd was growing quiet as the number continued its upward climb.

"Henry," Una pulled on his shirtsleeve, but he continued on.

"Fifteen," Henry called. A wave of desire swept over Una. He was growing in confidence, moving forward, and protecting her sister.

Horace turned and looked at Henry. The instinct to see Horace's jovial manner turn so completely was so powerful that Una's breath grew hard. His eyes blazed with frustration and curiosity. He gave a little smile of good humor to Henry, then pulled out his wallet and counted out all of his bills. He held the pile high above his head and called out to the room, "Twenty-seven forty-five."

Horace walked the pile up toward the stage.

McKenna looked at the man walking toward her. Una was about to walk behind him to take her sister off the stage and physically remove her from that man.

But Una didn't have to move because Henry was just as fast. He pulled out his own wallet and held the small item over his head.

"Thirty dollars," he called. McKenna gasped and dropped her basket, then quickly tried to bend and pick it up, only to push it further away from herself. The crowd seemed to be holding one collective breath.

Horace stopped walking and stood like a statue, not going forward and not going back, the wad of cash still in his hand.

There was a long pause. The auctioneer looked at Horace for a long while as a small cloud of fear entered his face.

"I guess we have our winner," the auctioneer said as he looked to Henry. McKenna stood unsteadily with her basket back in her hand. She looked from Horace to Henry, and then her eyes met Una's. Una smiled, and the smallest sliver of relief showed in McKenna's face. "Sold, to Henry Mackey for thirty dollars."

The crowd went up in a cheer, and Henry walked the cash forward. McKenna moved away as fast as she could into the crowd where a group of young girls McKenna's age surrounded her. Una smiled.

Una watched Henry's back with awe. What had just happened? Had Henry really just done that? For her? For her sister?

She watched Henry pick up the basket. He gave a little bow of his head to McKenna as he walked by the girls who all giggled. Then he kept walking back toward Una.

Una swallowed. Her basket was supposed to go up soon, but she didn't care. Una turned and walked through the crowd and out the main doors.

When she made it outside, she sucked in the fresh, night air. She felt like she was choking in there. Suffocating. She was afraid for herself, afraid of what she felt for that man. Afraid of the desire that overcame her. The heat that began afresh each time he looked at her.

Her neck was sweaty. Una ran her hand across it. She stumbled around the building, pressing her hand to the cool wood to keep her steady. When she stopped, she put her back to the wall and her basket on the ground.

There was a breath behind her. Her skin prickled from her feet all the way up to her neck.

"Una," Henry's resonant voice came from behind her. Una longed to be wrapped in that voice. She felt like he touched her with that voice.

His cool hand touched her neck, and she let her head lean back onto his hand. It was one small point of contact, but her skin burst with the feeling of it. She moved her head around until her cheek touched his hand. She turned again until her lips touched his hand. She pressed them into his skin, tasting him, needing him. Everything in her was pressing her to go further, to consume this man.

When her lips left Henry's hand, she pulled it into her hands. Her fingers kneaded into his soft flesh. She turned his wrist over and kissed the inside where his pulse beat out to her. Her lips moved to his neck, and she tasted him, drank him in. Her body moved forward, prodding her on, pushing her closer. She wanted to be wrapped in him, to be eclipsed within his body.

Then, with a force she was not expecting, her lips met his. He pulled back to look at her face, but Una did not want to let go. She held his lips securely in her own. She craved him too much not to have him.

With a show of strength she hadn't possessed moments before, Una pulled back so her face was three inches from his. Her breath was hard, and her eyes were hungry.

"You—" Henry looked over her face with a question. "Do you want to stop?"

Una tried desperately to pull her mind back to sanity. She needed to think clearly now. She needed…

"No," Una's chest heaved as she pressed herself to him.

Chapter Fifteen

Una's chest lifted with a hot breath as she looked into Henry's eyes. A tingling sensation had begun to move in waves through her body, and she felt a sudden longing to be closer to him; a longing to touch him, to have him touch her. Her cravings were both scary and electric—far beyond anything she'd felt before.

There was a small dip in the sidewall of the town hall only feet from where Una and Henry stood. They were pressed up against the wood planking in plain sight of anyone who might walk in past this way.

Una's lips found his, and she prodded him in the direction of the alcove. When he noticed her motion and where it led, he moved her until they were tucked back into the small recess. It was darker there, with the walls creating thick shadows from the moonlight.

Henry's hands clung to Una's body. He moved them around her bodice, around the back of her body, around the curve of her hips. He felt her like a curious child but with the hunger of a starved man.

Una pulled his bottom lip into her mouth between her teeth. She felt like she was being overwhelmed by sensation. A small gasp escaped her throat, and Henry's hand went to her mouth.

He opened his mouth as if about to say something, but he changed his mind, moved his hand, and brought his lips to hers instead.

A chill breeze cut through the thin material of her bloomers as Henry pulled the hem of her dress up to her calves. He pulled his face back and studied her with a sudden look of panic; a look that told her that he hadn't meant to do it, hadn't meant to begin a motion that might lead to something so definitive.

Una stared into his eyes for a long moment. Her heart was telling her one thing, and her mind was telling her another. She licked the taste of Henry off her lips. Her fingertips moved to his face and traced the outline of his jaw, nose, and forehead. He was beautiful, and the look in his eyes told her that he was hers.

"Una," Henry said her name as a plea, and she understood it perfectly. Her heart pounded a response to him. Henry's eyes penetrated into hers, and she felt a violent shiver run through her spine. The shiver pushed her body harder into his, causing another violent reaction of desire from the pit of her stomach.

A tear fell, rolling down her cheek, and Una watched Henry's eyes light up with worry again.

"Are you okay? We can stop," He instinctively backed away.

"No, please don't." She pulled him back to her. "I love this, I just—I never thought I would feel—happiness like this again."

The momentary panic on Henry's face melted, and he leaned forward, kissing the tear away from her cheek, and then kissing each eye.

"You deserve to feel happiness like this every day of your life. You deserve everything—I only wish I could—"

Una cut off his words by putting her lips to his mouth. She knew how his words were meant to end, and she didn't want to hear that. What she wanted was right in front of her.

Henry responded immediately, his body meeting hers. She sucked in another breath as together they lowered, then finally collapsed on top of one another, to the ground. The ground was covered in small stones, dirt, and flecks of hay and grass, but Una didn't care. One small stone pushed sharply into her back, but Una didn't mind that either. It meant that she was here. She was in Henry's arms. And it felt good.

Henry's hand brushed down to her skirts. Tentatively he began to pull them up. Once he realized that she wasn't interested in resisting, his need returned, and his hand squeezed her leg.

The desire that had been building was now crushing down on Una, knocking her breath from her lungs, demanding more. She'd never been dominated by such intense desire before. She'd never known anything could feel so necessary. She slid the thin white material from her legs and felt the night air hit her bare skin.

Her neck dropped back as Henry's fingers moved along the inside of her thigh. Her body was responding in ways that at first worried her, and then pulled at her until yet another new sensation was teasing her.

"Wait," Una looked up. A small spec of apprehension crept under her abandon. "I've—I've never done this before. I don't—I'm not sure I know…"

In response, Henry's fingers moved along her thigh until they came to the meeting of her legs. Una sucked in a quick violent breath. The movement of his fingers erased any thought other than the ones it was creating.

"There's nothing you need to know, you only need to feel… We'll go slowly. If you want to, at any time, you can tell me to stop."

His finger slid over her harder and a moist burst of arousal shot through her body.

"Don't stop," the words came out in spasms.

"Then I won't," Henry's fingers explored Una. There was the sound of people, thumping boots, and someone singing, from inside the building. The cluster of sounds were so close to her head, but somehow they seemed oceans away. Her hips lifted in response to Henry's touch, and every part of her body was asking for more. She didn't even know what it was that she wanted more of.

Then Henry's finger slid into her, and all at once, she let any residual guilt go. How could she feel guilty about something that felt so good? About something that seemed so perfect between the two of them?

His body lifted, and Una's fingers moved with Henry's as he unfastened his trousers. She felt the warmth of his skin underneath the cloth, and it felt like the most delicious secret. She moved her hand along him, looking at him with the same curiosity he'd had with her. She felt with awe the growing tension in his body. She breathed in heavily while turning her gaze up at him.

Half of his face was lit up in a stray shaft of moonlight, and Una watched his eyes and mouth as he moved. Slowly, carefully, Henry entered her. He watched her face for signs of pain as he went. Una tried to pretend that there was no pain. It wasn't what she expected. She'd assumed a feeling like the one his fingers had created, but this was different.

He moved slowly and with care. Her body gave resistance, and she felt every movement acutely. Then, with his next push forward, something in her gave way. Her body had accepted him, and she found herself able to relax around him. As he continued, the pain went away. After that, the first overwhelming sensations of desire and pleasure returned.

Henry had been watching her face and measuring her responses. He intuitively understood the responses in her face and body. As she began to enjoy him more, he became less inhibited, moving with abandon.

Her body responded to his. She lifted and mirrored his rhythms. The swell of her increasing craving was overcoming her senses. She moved her hands to his neck, down his back and gripped the sides of his ribcage. Her naked legs wrapped around his body, hugging him to her, pulling him in deeper, moving him closer to the core of her.

A pulsing and a growing plea had begun to move deep within her. There lay a blossoming anticipation of something about to explode, to overpower her very being.

Sweat glistened on Henry's brow, and Una could see the same, identical need appear behind his eyes, within his face, even in the tension of his body.

Her lips parted as her breath refused to be controlled any longer. Her throat dragged on the air it took in, her cheeks were burning red, and heat rolled down her body.

Una closed her eyes and opened them again. She felt the edge of her control fading, the sensation was coming to overwhelm her. She pulled in one more breath, released her own power, and let the crashing sensations slam down over her body. Her muscles jerked, and her eyes held Henry's as his mouth opened to a silent moan.

The two were locked in a tight frenzy of throbbing vibrations. Una's legs held Henry tightly, and his arms gripped her body in the same vital way.

After a long while, when there was only the sound of their breath, the muted sounds of the bidding from indoors, and the occasional horse snorts and foot stamps, Henry let his body slide over to the side of Una and lay back on the bare ground.

Quickly, she moved her skirts to cover her bare legs and sat up. She pulled at strands of straw and dirt that were stuck in her hair, used her hand to brush her clothing free of the ground. When Una looked down as she slid on her bloomers, she let out a small gasp.

Henry sat up fast, glimpsing the spot of blood on her white petticoat. She pulled her skirt over it.

"It's okay," he exhaled with relief. "I thought there might be... I don't know what. That," he looked to the now-covered spot where the blood had been, "is perfectly normal."

"Oh," Una furrowed her brow. How had she not learned this from her family? From her mother? The thought of her mother made her heart sink.

"What's wrong?" Henry's head dipped to see her eyes.

"Nothing. I was just thinking that—there are many things my mother hadn't yet told me."

Henry nodded in understanding. Una was thankful for his silence. Speaking of her mother out loud made her absence seem more real, and Una wanted the feeling and the sorrow to pass as soon as possible.

"Why don't we put ourselves together and go back inside?" He reached up and brushed a stray hair back from Una's face as he looked it over.

She nodded, and after he stood, she took his hand to get up.

"The green of that dress really does look beautiful on you," He admired her form as she brushed her dress down with her hands. She readjusted the folds of her skirt, and then turned to him for an inspection.

"Very decent," He smiled.

"I can't say the same for you," She gestured to his clothing. He was rumpled and rather looked like he'd been rolling around on the ground for a bit. "Here," She brushed him off and began to adjust his clothes as Henry watched her with a smile. "You could very easily do this yourself, you know."

"But I like watching you do it so much better," Henry grinned and turned around so that Una could brush off his back and adjust his clothes from the back as well.

By the time they walked back into the hall, the din had become a dull roar. There were lots of incriminating whispers being pelted about, and Una heard Horace's name mentioned from one group of older women. She turned to look at them only to find one of them looking at her, and then quickly turning back into the circle. How long would it take for both her and her sister to be considered part of the town? Probably not until they both had children and local husbands, and even then, they may always be foreigners.

Una turned and looked at all the female heads for her sister, but there was no bright red hair to be seen. She also looked around for Catherine but didn't see her either. Una tried to estimate how longed she'd been outside with Henry, but it was useless. She felt like everything at the party should have been going on the same as it had been, but she could feel that the mood had changed. It must have been altered by the Henry and Horace showdown.

"I don't see anyone," Una went up on tiptoe, but it didn't seem to matter as much since the hall had cleared out a good deal. People had designed themselves into circles and groups, and each seemed to be having its own retelling of the bid on McKenna's basket.

"Oh dear," Una said as she bit down on her lip. Could Catherine have gotten mad at McKenna and taken her home? Or maybe McKenna went off with that group of girls, Una didn't see any of them either. It was clear that tonight's event was not going to be as long and rowdy as the dance had been only a week earlier. This was either the way it was or the way it had become since Horace hadn't gotten his way.

"I thought this was what you wanted? A big fuss over the bid to get Horace all wound up?" Henry seemed to be reading Una's thoughts, and he felt things were a lot less serious than Una did. He seemed relaxed and happy. Just seeing a smile tweak at the edges of his mouth made Una want to kiss him again.

Una scrunched her brow, "I guess I did."

"Well, it worked." Henry nodded toward another end of the room where Horace was seated with the girl he'd danced with last week. The girl was sitting on his lap. Another, similarly dressed woman, stood by his side, and yet another next to a man that was talking and laughing just as loudly as Horace was.

"We should go. I don't see your brother, my sister, or either of the Donnellys." Una's heart was beginning to beat like a strong hammer, the sort of hammer that realizes they might have been looking for her. And they might have been looking for Henry.

They could have all just decided that the night was going poorly and that they should go home. McKenna could be with Saul for all Una knew. Or they may all have put it together about Una and Henry. It wouldn't be too difficult.

Henry, once again, must have understood what was going through Una's mind because he put a hand on her wrist. Una immediately looked around to see if anyone was watching them, if anyone could have seen the gesture.

"It's okay," he said, his voice soft and gentle. "No one is looking. Everything will be okay." He released her wrist and nodded toward the door. "Let's go outside again, see if their wagons are still here. We'll know more then."

There was a crack from the other side of the room, and Una turned around to see Horace red in the face. He'd thrown a glass on the floor, and the women around him all gave little screams of surprise. The room went quiet. At first, Una thought the reaction was a result of Horace seeing Henry. When she looked, Una was relieved to see that the tantrum was about something the other man had said or maybe even one of the women. The two men seemed to be locked in some sort of heated argument. Una had never heard Horace speak in such constrained and understated tones.

"What do you think that's about?" Una whispered to Henry who was pushing her gently toward the door.

"I'm not sure, but I don't think I want to be around if Horace is in a bad way. I am the one who outbid him, if you will remember."

Una, remembering her first instinct of who the smashed glass was about, turned fully and began walking with more purpose out of the hall "Good point," she said.

Once they were outside, there was no sign on Saul's carriage, nor of the Donnelly family carriage, and no sign of McKenna herself.

"Does that mean everyone's gone home?" Una's palms felt sweaty, and she was beginning to wish that she were safely back in the children's room above the Donnelly's main room.

"I'd better take you home too," Henry said as he turned toward his own wagon.

"What will I tell them?"

"That you felt ill? That…" He helped Una onto the carriage and then walked around to his own seat. "I guess you could say that you found me and asked me to take you home."

Una nodded. It didn't sound as promising as she'd hoped, but she couldn't think of anything better.

Chapter Sixteen

Una insisted on being let off away from the house so the wheels of Henry's wagon wouldn't wake the family. She wasn't sure how well she would lie tonight if confronted by Catherine. She just wanted to be in bed curled up next to her sister.

Henry jumped down from his seat as Una got down from hers on the other side.

"You can't come with me. What if one of them sees you?" She walked toward Henry, who put his hand to her cheek.

"I suppose we've had enough risk for one night. But," he looked at her with serious eyes, "I don't want this to be the end of us. It can't be."

Una had been avoiding the thoughts of what would come next, and now her heart thudded against her ears. In many ways, they were the words she wanted to hear, but they also weren't sensible. Despite the sensible advisements her brain was giving out, a small tug of hope began pulling at her, and a part of her began to believe that maybe that part of her was wrong. Maybe there was something more. Something she didn't know yet.

"Is there…" Una's voice trembled, and she found that she was scared to ask the question. She was scared to know Henry's intentions, or the possibility of them coming to fruition even if his intentions were for her. "I know your brother is getting the farm, Catherine has told us that." Una rubbed her lips together and looked to the sky. "She said you were saving for your own farm?"

"I am," He put both of his hands on her shoulders. His face was earnest, but she could see a struggle beaming out behind his eyes. "It will be awhile yet. I… don't have everything I need. Before I met you I was planning on staying with Saul for the next three years…" he sighed, "maybe even five years depending on the harvests, to save what I would need. Unless…" His voice faded off, and he looked up to the sky just as she had done a moment before.

"Unless you married a girl who had money?" Una finished his thought, and a pained expression crossed his face. "I understand," She braced herself quickly and tried to sound as nonchalant as she could. "That's usual enough."

Henry stared at Una, and she walked slowly around the wagon trying to compose herself before she looked at his face again.

"Catherine wants us out of her house soon. She says she can't afford to keep us both much longer. She also says that Saul and Horace had agreed to reimburse her for our expenses." Una found this hard to say so she said it as she looked to the ground.

Henry didn't say anything for a long time.

"I guess you'd better be getting back." He said. He was staring in the direction of the Donnelly house, and Una's heart sank. The flutter of hope disappeared, and a swelling of deep-rooted pain began to blossom inside of her. This was what she had expected. She'd gone through too much to assume life would be... To assume that there would be some sort of happy ending waiting in the future.

"Yes, of course, I'd better," She tried to smile, but it didn't work. "It's late and someone may still be up."

Henry nodded. Una turned toward the house and took two steps forward before spinning around and running hard into Henry's arms. Her lips pushed against his. There was a desperation behind her kiss, a need that could never be met.

Then just as suddenly as she'd kissed him, she turned and walked back toward the house. She thought she could feel Henry's eyes on her, but she couldn't make herself turn around to look. He was hers, she thought, and she kept repeating the words in her mind. It needed repeating because it couldn't be true. He couldn't be hers. For now, yes, but soon she would have to marry Saul, and eventually Henry would realize how beautiful Cecily or some other girl was.

Even as she thought it, she knew it wasn't true. Though she'd never experienced anything like it before, she knew what they had was unique. Permanent. It may not be what they would get to live, but it would always be the truth.

The short walk helped clear her mind and stiffen her spine for any possible run-in with a family member at the house.

There didn't seem to be anyone awake, so Una carefully opened the front door and closed it softly behind her. As she moved into the room with only the faintest glow of a smoldering fire, she saw Catherine. The older woman was sitting in a chair looking out blankly in front of her.

Una looked quickly at the front window, wondering briefly if she'd been able to see anything. Quickly she remembered how hidden the wagon had been from the front of the house and thought how absurd the idea was. Even with the sensible knowledge of it, Una still felt like Catherine knew. Perhaps that everyone knew.

"Hi," Her own sound of surprise betrayed Una.

Catherine didn't say anything for a while but studied her. Una took that as a sign and made a step forward to go up the stairs and to bed.

"Where were you tonight?" Catherine's voice was low and clear. Una's foot stopped mid-step, and she felt her body turn to marble.

"Sick," Una said immediately. It had come out too fast. "I think it was the air in the hall. It was so stuffy tonight, wasn't it?" She tried to backpedal and make herself sound more believable.

"We looked for you." Catherine's stony face and hard voice told Una everything she needed to know. "We couldn't find you. Or your sister either."

This last bit set a fire of panic into Una's heart. She hadn't been expecting that. "Oh," Una's brows creased. "Is… did she come home with you?" The image of McKenna sitting all alone at the hall was enough to make Una want to turn and run back as quickly as possible.

"It turns out she was sick too," Catherine tapped her foot on the floor. "Must be a Brady thing."

"But she's here?" Una was losing her patience with Catherine but kept herself reined in.

"In bed."

McKenna was sick? Una looked to the stairway, ready to run up it and see her sister.

"Maybe it was the pie?" Catherine said from behind her. Una's mind began to roll through the statement, and then landed flatly on the answer. The pie. She'd forgotten all about the pie. The salt she'd shoveled in before putting the filling on top. Catherine and Joseph had one of those pies.

Una turned slowly, "The pie?" Her voice was too innocent, and Una wanted to pinch herself. She'd been reacting to everything all wrong. Everything Catherine said was met with the worst possible response from Una.

"Or didn't you eat any?" Catherine's body bristled, and she shifted in her chair. The two women stared at each other, Una not even pretending innocence any longer. "The bidding stopped while you were… sick. I don't see your basket though?"

Una's hands clenched. She'd forgotten all about her basket. She'd put it down somewhere, but where?

"I—I gave it to Henry to give to Saul." Una stammered out. She was surprised when Catherine seemed to take this as a legitimate answer.

"Well, someone ought to tell him not to eat the pie." Her expression soured again. "I suppose he'll find out soon enough either way." Una tried to give her another innocent and repentant expression, but again it felt as if she'd fallen flat.

"Well, go on upstairs, then," Catherine finally said as if she was repulsed by the sight of her. Una didn't care if she was. She turned and quietly, so as not to wake any more of the family, climbed the stairs to her room.

Everything was dark, but two long beams of moonlight crept along the floor. Una walked delicately over to her sister, putting her hand to her forehead. McKenna did feel hot. For a brief moment Una thought of going back downstairs to ask about a doctor but decided not to. The doctor would probably be drunk tonight anyway. Una quietly undressed, hiding her petticoats that would need to be cleaned in the morning. Then she went to the washbasin and wet a cloth.

Una pressed the cloth to her sister's forehead and watched McKenna's translucent eyelids flicker. Una let her hand push McKenna's hair back away from her face. She hadn't meant to wake her, but the sight of McKenna's large eyes made Una feel better.

"Where were you?" McKenna whispered with her voice full of sleep.

Una leaned over and kissed McKenna on the forehead. "How are you feeling?"

"Better, now that you're here," McKenna smiled. Una felt a surge of guilt. She should have been there for her sister. Young McKenna had been left to Catherine and the rest of the town after Henry's display and Horace's disdain while Una had been…while Una had been with Henry. Her mind slid easily into the feel of Henry's hands, the feel of his body on top of hers, the feel of his eyes on hers. It took some effort to push the thoughts and feelings away and focus back on her sister. It was impossible to regret anything that had happened with Henry. Besides, what was done was done, and now she was here with McKenna.

McKenna opened her mouth again, but Una put her fingers across her lips and shook her head gently, "We can talk tomorrow. Tonight we should sleep."

A curious expression crossed McKenna's face, but Una ignored it and crawled into bed.

Chapter Seventeen

The next morning, Una woke early to try and clean off her petticoat. The round splotch of blood had hardened in the night, and Una wondered if she would be able to clean it out at all without access to boiling water and soap. She could blame it on her menses if she had to and say that the sickness had really been cramps.

She scrubbed and washed in the freezing cold water as quietly as she could. They normally heated the water to wash everything properly, but then Catherine would be privy to everything washed. She might even be washing it herself now that Una had taken so definitively to the fields.

Unable to do any more, she wrung them out as well as she could and took them silently back to her room. It was impossible to discreetly hang them somewhere without someone noticing, so she decided to tuck them away wet until a better opportunity presented itself.

After that, the morning went off as usual. McKenna was feeling better. Una suspected that it had been a combination of anxiety and the heat and the air in the hall that had made her sister feel so ill. Una had warned her sister against having any more of the town's famous punch, and McKenna seemed to take this as good advice.

The younger children were bursting with energy and questions about the baskets and the bidding, but Una didn't have it in her to answer any of them. Catherine resumed her silent treatment to Una, but as it was becoming her normal behavior toward her, it didn't really bother Una any more.

Una worked with Joseph for a good part of the morning to repair some fencing that needed fixing before it fell apart. Three horses were kept inside the pen, and they came over to watch the progress being made on the fence in between their chomping and grazing. Una could see McKenna and the children from that vantage point and watched them playing with the animals.

McKenna was gentle and loving to each animal. She treated the goats like they were little children, and compared with little Joe, the goats weren't all that different. They both jumped around and sprang into action at random moments.

Once the horse fence was mended, they walked around to check the other wood planks and pens, reinforcing some when they found any that looked like they needed it. Una decided to go in for lunch and eat with the family. She'd been exhausting herself for days with her tireless work schedule, and she needed rest.

She looked out over the fields as she went back out after lunch and decided that the next morning she would begin work when Joseph began work, no sooner. She would end work when he ended work, no longer. And she would take all of her meals in the house with the others. Just the thought of it made her feel stronger. As she was walking out past the chicken coop, she heard a commotion of little voices. The children were yelling from outside to their parents inside.

Una turned and saw McKenna coming out of the house behind her. They began to hear the sound of carriage wheels, and Una understood what the children were yelling about. There was about to be company in the Donnelly house.

"Who do you think it is?" McKenna asked, looking to Una. Una was staring out around the house waiting for something to come into view on the road.

"I don't know," She took a few steps to the side so that she would have a better view around the house. They waited as the sounds of the wheels and the horses clomping got louder. Just before the carriage came into view, Una knew who it was. The broad, bold features and beautiful carriage rolled toward the Donnelly house. Horace Boucher.

"What does he want?" McKenna's voice was meek, and she physically wilted at the sight of him.

"I don't know. Maybe it has something to do with the basket bidding," Una said. Her skin prickled, and she knew that something was about to go very wrong. She shouldn't have pushed Henry to bid. Now maybe Horace wanted to get married sooner, immediately, this moment. He would want to prove to everyone just who got the girl in the end. Or maybe he was mad about it all and wanted… "What more could he possibly want?" Una wondered.

Joseph had been about to open the back door to come out for his afternoon work, but the door closed again, and he remained inside. Una took McKenna's hand and walked closer to the door.

"No, please," McKenna pulled back on Una's hand. "I don't want to go in, not today. Not after last night."

Una looked at her sister and nodded. She hadn't intended for them both to go in, but only to be closer to the house so they could hear what was going on. But, looking at her sister's face and the fear that streaked across it, Una understood that even this would be too much.

"Go along, then," Una smiled and released McKenna's hand. "Go tend to the animals—whatever you were going to do when we were on our way out here."

McKenna exhaled a shaky breath and looked relieved. She nodded vigorously, and then turned and ran off away from the house. Una turned back and walked the rest of the way by herself, the uneasiness growing more raucous as she went.

The back door was closed, but Horace had such a loud, clear voice that Una was sure she would be able to catch some, if not all, of what he said. She leaned back against the wall and listened to the footsteps inside, the clutter of voices, and the momentary silence of them all getting situated.

Either Horace hadn't sat down at all, or he'd gotten back to his feet because Una heard his loud, tromping footsteps once more.

"I was right to…trouble with Henry Mackey," Was the first thing she heard, and her heart pounded heavily. She missed little words as Horace's voice dipped in and out. Her ears tuned in, and she listened with a focus and intention she hadn't had possession of only a few minutes before.

"David was far from sober, but he saw what he saw."

There was a question from Catherine that Una couldn't hear. But the incredulity, annoyance, and panic were all clearly audible.

"Clear as day, he says, he saw them," Horace's voice was indignant and disgusted and easily overpowered the sentiment in Catherine's words.

Una pressed a hand to her face. What did this mean? The words were clanking together in her mind.

Someone saw her with Henry. Someone saw them. As the realization hit her, she had to clutch onto the house to keep from falling over. She replayed Horace's words over again in her mind, and then realized he was saying something else.

"I've already cancelled the arrangements, told the pastor the wedding is off." There was the sound of Horace's boots on the wooden floor again. "You needn't try to change my mind, I'll find someone else fast enough."

There was the sound of chairs, Catherine's voice, "Horace, I know that this is some sort of—"

"She's a whore. Just a common whore—" This time Horace's voice barked the words so loudly that Una had to take a step back. "I consider you responsible for this. You were the one who set this up, and they are your family. If I were you, I would send them back to where they came from."

The door slammed, and there were muted sounds of Catherine and Joseph talking between themselves. Una took two steps away from the house. She needed to get to the fields, but her legs didn't feel like they were working. What about her petticoat? It would just be evidence to what Horace said.

So he'd decided that McKenna was tainted because of what she'd done? Horace was out of the way, but what about another man? Would this always be attached to McKenna just as it would be to Una?

Una stumbled toward the barn. She was feeling sick. Her mind was spinning with ways to fix this. If the man was drunk then—well, then couldn't she just deny it? Couldn't they both? What about Henry? What about Saul? Tears sprang to Una's eyes as she thought of what this might mean.

Picking up the tools that she had been planning to use, she tried to make her body move out of the barn and toward the fields. As soon as her foot stepped out into the open, she saw Joseph. Una stopped.

"I think it's best if you come in now," Joseph said. His eyes looked sad, and Una felt a pang of guilt for hurting this man. Catherine was difficult, but Joseph had been kind enough to open his house to them, and now she'd disgraced his family's name. "You'd best be bringing your sister too."

Una nodded but didn't move. Joseph turned and walked back to the house. Una waited until the door closed behind him to turn and look for McKenna.

As poorly as McKenna had looked only a few minutes ago when she'd seen Horace coming, she looked perfectly at ease with the cow and her new baby. Una watched her for a long moment, not wanting to interrupt her sister with bad news. Una was embarrassed for herself. Embarrassed to set such an example for McKenna. She knew that their parents would never approve of such behavior, but her parents were no longer alive.

Una took a deep breath, "McKenna."

Her sister's bright red head turned to Una. The look of worry that Una had seen before on McKenna returned now. "We're wanted in the house."

McKenna let her hand slide along the calf's downy back before stepping away from the animals and walking toward her sister.

"He wants to see me?" McKenna's voice was shaky.

Una shook her head, happy to at least assuage one fear, "No. He's not here anymore."

"Then what's wrong?" McKenna was trying to build her strength up, and she walked a little taller.

Una opened her mouth but couldn't say anything. How could she tell her sister this? How could she explain?

"You don't have to marry Horace anymore," Una said instead. McKenna's breath quickened.

"Why? Because of Henry? Because of the bidding?" McKenna's words were growing with an excitement that seemed to only pick up. "Are they very mad? The Donnellys?"

Una opened her mouth again but just nodded instead. If there was one very good thing about all this, it was that McKenna would not be marrying Horace. For that, Una could be thankful. However, even that felt like a very small victory compared with such a big loss looming overhead.

Una put an arm around her sister and pulled her small body in closer to her own.

"Are you okay? You're shaking." McKenna stopped walking.

"I'm just," Una searched for some excuse, but since the truth was waiting only moments away, it seemed ridiculous to even try. "Let's just go inside."

McKenna nodded, and her momentary lift of spirit quickly turned. The two sisters walked silently and slowly to the house. Una seemed to notice things she'd never noticed before. She noticed how green the patch of grass next to the house was. How the wind blew into their faces and carried the scent of wood and fire. She felt the place where McKenna's shoulder bone went into its socket. She noticed now, more than ever, how close the house was to the barn and animal pens. Things were so much more condensed here than they had been on her family's land in Ireland. In Ireland, they'd had a large plot of land to grow and raise animals. This was small in comparison, yet here the Donnellys were so much richer.

Catherine swung around when Una walked through the back door. She'd gone in before McKenna, hoping to take the brunt of the shaming that she certainly deserved. Una was ready for an attack, ready for threats, even ready to be kicked out.

A scary thought struck Una in that moment with the other woman's eyes on her. What if Catherine had been right all along? That security was more important than anything else? Now, Una had taken away any security that McKenna might have had. When it came down to the essentials, to food, shelter, water, a place to sleep at night, Horace seemed less of a monster.

"Sit," Catherine's voice was steely. Both girls walked across the room to the seats where Catherine's thin finger was pointing. "I'm sure you know that Horace Boucher was just here." She looked at both girls, but neither said anything. Catherine's words hadn't come across as a question, yet she stared them down as if waiting for an answer.

"Well, he did," She continued as she released a sigh into the room. "It seems that someone from town saw you…" Catherine thought over her words, "with Henry last night." Catherine turned, and Una tried to think of a way to respond, a way to justify her actions, but with a sudden shock she realized that Catherine was looking at McKenna. Una turned to McKenna too and saw her sister's face go white and her eyes open wide.

"With Henry—" McKenna repeated the words though Una could tell that her sister wasn't sure what they meant. "You mean the basket?"

"Yes," Catherine put both of her hands on her hips. Una looked to Joseph, who seemed more than embarrassed by their conversation. His eyes seemed to be following some invisible shape on the floor. "Of course, the whole town saw you and him and the basket episode… and then after the basket."

"After the basket?" McKenna looked to Una, and then back to Catherine. "After the basket? I don't think I understand."

"What happened after the bidding?" Catherine prodded.

"I talked to some girls."

Catherine made a hand motion for McKenna to keep going.

"Then I was sick, I felt…I told you last night."

Catherine nodded her head as if those words proved everything. "He's a handsome boy. It must be very flattering for a young girl like you to have him bid on you like that. Against the likes of Horace Boucher, no less."

McKenna seemed to start understanding Catherine's words, and the severity of their meaning, "I would never do that. I would never."

"Someone *saw* you. After Henry made a fool of himself buying your basket, they saw you together. Outside, in the moonlight. They say you were doing more than just talking too." Catherine shook her head in a tired way. "You in that green dress."

There was a silence as the words slipped out into the room. Catherine stared blankly at McKenna, and then slowly turned her eyes to Una.

Chapter Eighteen

Una's mind had been whirling ever since she realized that Horace had come to tell Catherine and Joseph about McKenna, not about her. It seemed so preposterous to her, that at first she doubted they could think it even potentially true. But the more Catherine spoke, the more Una understood that Catherine genuinely thought that McKenna had truly been the one with Henry the night before.

And what exactly had the man said they were doing? Did "under the moonlight" mean they were still on the side of the hall kissing? Or did it mean that he'd seen them— Una could barely finish the thought, it was so horrifying.

Since Catherine had been talking, she'd not been able to open her mouth for a moment before her mind started rattling away again. At first, Una's mind struck on the thought that at least if McKenna were the one blamed, then she would not marry Horace, or more accurately, Horace would not marry her. On the other hand, Una didn't want any shame or harm to fall on McKenna, and Una knew that her sister would take such an accusation very badly.

Una went back and forth in her mind until the words, "…green dress," floated out into the air. As Catherine's eyes moved to Una, there was nothing more to think about. Catherine knew. Catherine's eyes said it all. She understood exactly what had happened.

Catherine's chest heaved with her breath, and she looked from one sister to the other. "I knew it was a bad idea to take you in."

Joseph's head lifted in surprise at Catherine's words. Catherine noticed the movement and turned to her husband.

"Perhaps we'd better talk alone," Catherine said, indicating the three women. "I'm afraid we have some womanly things to talk over that might make you uncomfortable."

Joseph's face turned scarlet, and his eyes refused to move in the direction of either Brady sister. He stood abruptly, "Yes, of course. I have work. I should," He muttered the entire walk out of the house, probably hoping no one would say anything until he was gone and his mutterings had stopped. When the door closed behind him, there was a silence that hung over all three women.

"McKenna, will you make sure the younger children are all away from the house and that they stay away?" Catherine's voice was nice. Too nice. McKenna stood and looked to Una with a scared look in her eyes, and then walked to the front door and stepped outside.

As soon as McKenna was gone, Catherine's focus was back on Una.

"Who drove you home last night? I heard wheels, but I didn't see anyone." Her voice was barely a whisper, and the veins in her necks lifted up like ropes held taut.

Una straightened her spine and tried to gather all her available courage together.

She licked her lips, "Henry did."

Catherine didn't nod or say anything, but the look in her eyes said what her words didn't.

"Where did you go while you were *sick* last night?" Catherine's voice was still tight but louder than before.

Una exhaled. "I will tell you freely that the man Horace was talking about saw me. Not McKenna."

Catherine blew out a breath and closed her eyes. When she opened them again, she wasn't looking at Una.

There was a crushing silence as Catherine walked to the window and then back, preoccupied with her own thoughts.

"Please," Una began. "McKenna can't marry that man. We must clear her name, but she can't go back to Horace. There has to be someone else… or maybe, maybe she could help you with the children for a few years? I would leave—"

"You will not leave." Catherine stopped her walking and turned her focus back to Una. "You've already won with Horace. He's too stubborn. Even if we went to him with the truth, he would never take McKenna back. People would never believe it anyway. They would just think you were protecting your younger sister." Catherine looked up, "No. Not after Henry's stunt buying her basket last night. Everyone was talking about it last night and certainly will be today. Now they'll have another piece of gossip to go with it." Catherine paused, "Horace is not a discreet man."

Una cringed. She'd caused all of this. How had things gone so incredibly wrong from something so beautiful?

"I suppose you put Henry up to buy McKenna's basket as well?" Catherine asked Una.

Una thought about the question and decided that there was no point in holding anything else back, so she nodded.

"Well, you've made a real mess of things. That is certain."

Una mentally agreed with Catherine. She had made a mess of things. There was certainly no denying that. It seemed that it was all in Catherine's hands now, and Catherine knew it. Catherine was piecing things together in her mind and occasionally made little sounds as she worked out things. Since she had no solutions herself, Una had no option but to wait.

"This is what we will do." Catherine folded her hands together and looked straight at Una. "You will marry Saul." Before Una could say anything, Catherine continued, "That is the only answer. Saul will still have you, even with a disgraced sister. It will have to happen soon, immediately. You can't stay here any longer, not with this hanging over your heads. People will begin to associate my girls with this behavior, and they will be at marrying age soon themselves." Catherine looked defensively at Una, "I have to think of my girls first."

Una closed her eyes and pressed her fingertips to them before looking at Catherine again. "I'm sorry for your girls, and to have put you in such a... bad position." Una was sincere. She wasn't sorry about her night with Henry, but she was sorry for the situation it was putting them in. She was sorry that she hadn't had more sense in the moment. She was sorry that she couldn't run off and marry him right now. She was also sorry that it might possibly make Catherine or her family look bad when they had gone to such trouble for both her and her sister.

"The other piece of the puzzle is, of course, McKenna."

Una bristled at the mention of her sister.

"...McKenna will have to marry Henry," Catherine finished the train of thought. "It's the only solution. Saul will pay both of your expenses. You will both be provided for, and her name might be saved."

Una's skin chilled. She didn't like Catherine's plan. She probably wouldn't like any plan, but Catherine's plan was out of the question. First of all, Una couldn't possibly let McKenna take any responsibility for something Una had done, even if the rest of the town didn't believe a word of it. She would just have to convince them. She wouldn't let McKenna marry Horace no matter what, but the thought of her sister marrying the man that she loved while Una married someone else was... it made Una's skin crawl. This was all becoming too much, and she could read in Catherine's eyes that she wanted it done now. Tonight. Tomorrow. As soon as it could be done.

Una stood. She realized that Catherine had been watching her, and the older woman now put up a hand to stop Una from speaking.

"I know what you think, and I know what you're going to say. But listen to me." She gestured for Una to sit back down. Una thought about her options and decided to let Catherine have her say before telling her what would and would not happen in the next few days.

"You love your sister, don't you?"

Una frowned and said, "Of course I do. That's why I can't let her take the blame for all of this."

"Who will really be punished by my plan though? Your sister?" Catherine stepped closer and sat across from Una. "If your sister marries Henry, then her transgression, though remembered, will not be harshly met. It is only you and Henry who would be punished as you would each have to give the other up."

Una looked around the room as an uncomfortable feeling crept over her.

"McKenna would be well looked after with Henry. He would treat her well, he would be a good husband, they would soon have children, and eventually he would forget what he felt for you." Catherine held up a hand in anticipation of a response from Una. "You would be providing your sister with a good life. A better life than any of the alternatives."

The uncomfortable feeling grew. It was, in part, a truth. It was true that in the moment, a secure home, a good, loving husband, food on her plate, and a place to sleep, made up the best possible outcome for McKenna. If Una took her sister and left in the night, they would have nothing. She couldn't do that to McKenna, not after all they'd been through to get here—the days of not eating, illness, and death everywhere. How could Una possibly let her sister risk that all over again? At least with Henry McKenna, she was guaranteed a good man, a man who would care for her, someone who was the opposite of a man like Horace.

There was the stark reality to face. There was no way for Henry to marry Una and provide for her and for her sister.

For an odd moment, Una thought she smelled the air that had clung to them on the ship as they travelled across the Atlantic. The smell of salt and seawater, the smell of human flesh, the smell of people who hadn't been washed in weeks. It was a desperate, hopeless smell. Una looked around her for the source of the scent, but it was gone. Perhaps it hadn't been real to begin with.

"I'm afraid you are out of choices," Catherine said. The words came from her mouth almost tenderly, but Una was not fooled. There was a hard part of Catherine. Una wasn't sure why she seemed to bring it out in the other woman, but there it was.

"And what is your answer?" Catherine leaned back in her chair as if she already knew the answer. "Will you protect your sister, or will you protect yourself?"

Chapter Nineteen

Una spent the rest of the day outside. She abandoned her work in the fields for the solace of the roads. She didn't have the energy to see or talk to McKenna, so she slipped out of the door and down the road before anyone could notice. She walked for three hours, and when she began to walk toward the house again, she found the tree where she'd sat with McKenna, a time that now felt so long ago.

The land was really very beautiful in St. Joseph. Una felt like she had just begun to notice it. Her mind had been caught somewhere between the past of Ireland and the present since they'd left their homeland. America would always be her home now. She couldn't go back to Ireland. There was no one there for her, nothing there. She could continue west, she supposed, though she didn't know how she would pay for anything.

Una looked over the land. Food seemed to be springing from everywhere. A person need never go hungry in a land like this. It felt so malleable and fertile. But, Una knew the truth too. Ireland had been like that once too, but droughts, sickness, and barren, wasted land came to every town. Even in America. She tried to imagine this land void of life but found the task impossible.

Picking up a small branch that had fallen from the tree, Una followed the rough edges until it broke into two pieces in her hand. She looked at the broken end, at the green living pith and rubbed her thumb against it.

It had been under the branches of this tree where she and Henry had shared their first kiss. Her heart longed for that day now. Longed for the chance to freely give herself to Henry, to watch herself through his eyes. His beautiful green eyes. There were small flecks of gold mixed with the green. She could imagine them perfectly now.

A tear slid down her cheek, and Una quickly pushed it away. The tree felt strong and sturdy behind her back. So much stronger than she felt herself. Perhaps if she sat there long enough, the tree would eventually grow over her, and she would become part of the land.

Una threw the torn pieces of the branch to the ground and brushed her hands off on her dress. She had to stop her mind from wandering into the impossible. She had to figure out a solution that was real.

Una sat and thought until her mind wouldn't work anymore. The same solutions churned over and over again in her mind. When her limbs began to go numb from sitting in the same position for so long, she stood. She wouldn't be part of the tree today. It was time to go.

~

When she walked back into the Donnelly house, the family was seated for dinner. It seemed natural to Una to see Henry and Saul around the table as well. Catherine was a woman of her word. She was making her plans happen as quickly as possible.

The group stopped eating, and Una felt all eyes on her.

"I'm sorry to come in late... to interrupt." She barely felt as if she were the one speaking, but rather someone else that she herself was watching with interest.

Catherine's eyes flicked to the empty seat where Una should be moving to sit, but Una didn't move. She could feel Henry's eyes. They felt like they were piercing through her skin. It took all of her strength and will to keep from looking right back into his eyes and falling back into him again. She knew how easy it would be to get lost in Henry and to never climb out.

"I know this is very... I was hoping, Saul, if I could speak to you alone for a moment? After your dinner if you like. I don't want to interrupt, but it's lovely outside." Una didn't wait for a reply but turned to the door and went back outside.

Saul didn't wait for dinner to end but followed her immediately, and Una was grateful to him for that. She was tired of sitting with her thoughts. The only thing she could see now was action.

"Hello," Una said to Saul. She felt suddenly shy and scared for what she had to say. She took a few steps from the house and waited for Saul to follow her. Walking would be easier. She looked to the horizon and breathed her strength back into her again.

"There's something I need to tell you," Una said with her new strength showing in her voice. She turned and glanced at Saul, and then back to the horizon. "I guess you've heard about my sister and your brother?"

To Una's surprise, Saul didn't look uncomfortable at all. He nodded and wore a contemplative look she hadn't seen before.

"Catherine wants them to get married as soon as possible, and I… I agree." Una cleared her throat and let herself walk for a few more steps before trying to say anything else. "I know that Henry can't afford it now, but I was hoping… you would let them stay in your house until… until he can." She quickly turned to him. "I need you to promise me that you will take McKenna in as one of your own, that you will protect her like she is your sister."

She'd stopped walking, and Saul stopped too. He moved back a step to become parallel with Una. Saul evaluated Una for a moment and then nodded again, "Your sister will be welcome in my house. I swear it."

Una swallowed back the rising ball in her throat. It had been the most important thing she'd needed to hear. Una nodded and pressed her hands together.

"Saul, I can't marry you." Her words were blunt, but they had to be blunt, it was the only way. "I love someone else, and I always will. It wouldn't be fair to you, and it wouldn't be fair to me." She looked into his eyes. It felt like someone was pulling off her fingernails to say something that might hurt this gentle giant. Saul seemed like a good man, a nice man, and he didn't deserve this from her or anyone.

"I'm so sorry for letting this go on for so long." Una turned back to the horizon, "I'm leaving in the morning. McKenna will stay and marry Henry. She will be taken care of and that is the most important thing."

"Where will you go?" Saul's words were still quiet, but in the silence of the evening, they were clear and easy to understand. Una looked at him again.

"I don't know," she said, shaking her head lightly. There was no panic in it anymore for her. McKenna would be safe, and one day, McKenna would be loved by Henry. Perhaps one day Una could even come back to see her. The thought was short-lived, flitting through Una's mind before being pushed away. There would be no coming back.

Saul put his hands in his pockets as they turned to return to the house. "Do you—will you need some money? I mean do you have any?"

Una turned to him with fresh eyes. It was the first time they'd been able to speak to each other with her understanding him. She had just told him that she was breaking her commitment to marry him because she was in love with someone else, and he was asking if she had any money, if she would be ok. It felt surreal, and his kindness was not lost on her.

"I'll be okay. As long as McKenna is okay, I'll be fine." They walked in silence for a moment. "Before this, before America, we'd both been through something much worse. I don't think anything could ever be as hard again."

Just before they got to the front porch, Una turned to Saul once more.

"There's one more thing."

Saul didn't say anything but looked at her in a way that told her he was listening.

"If you could not say anything to anyone until after I'm gone. Everyone will know tomorrow, I'm sure. If you could just wait until then?"

Saul nodded in his quiet way, and the two walked back into the house.

When they walked in, the table had dispersed, and everyone was sitting in front of the fire. Just as they had before, the group stopped their activities and conversation to stare at the two people coming in. Saul moved to a seat near Henry, and Una stayed where she was.

"I'm not feeling well tonight. If you all will be so good as to excuse me." She dipped her head the slightest bit, and despite her best intentions, her eyes met Henry's. The depth of his feeling and communication in one glance was enough to knock her over. Una took a step back and caught the emotions that were rising in her chest. Her eyes darted away, accidentally colliding with Catherine's gaze, and then fell back to Henry.

Una turned on her heel and ran up the stairs to her room. She slid onto the small bed she shared with her sister and stared at the wall.

Tears slid down Una's face, and her body shook. She opened her mouth and poured out her silent cry.

Chapter Twenty

Una couldn't sleep, not that she wanted to. It was too dangerous to fall asleep. She let herself feel the weight of her sister crawling into bed next to her, knowing it would be for the last time. The night felt like it was moving so quickly. Every new moment was one she wanted to spend next to her sister. She wanted to feel her breathing and know that she was safe.

When McKenna's body began the deep, steady breath of sleep, Una turned and watched her sister's face. She wanted to keep the picture of it with her always. Wherever she would go, whenever she would be about to fall asleep, she would think of her sister's sleeping face.

It seemed impossible that this could be the last time she might see sister outside of her memory. Every time the thought sprang up, Una felt a new swell of tears cloud her eyes.

Una had left all her other family buried in the ground in Ireland, yet this was the hardest thing she would ever do. Una had told herself over and over again as they left, as they came to a new country, that this was the last time it would happen, that she would not have to separate so painfully again. She knew that one day McKenna would die, but Una fully intended for that day to come long after she herself was snuggly buried in the ground.

McKenna was alive. Henry was alive. Somehow she was now leaving them both forever. Every part of her plan was paralyzing to think about. It was impossible for her mind to avoid it. Her consciousness seemed to roll through circle after circle. The thoughts would come, but each time her mind crashed over it, she had to retreat away from it all until the thoughts sprang out once more.

Una hummed her mother's lullabies to her sister as she thought of them. The sound of her own voice helped to relax her, but the knowledge of what she shared with McKenna and McKenna alone stood between Una and the door.

When the house had been asleep for a long time and Una had run out of lullabies, she crept out of bed.

Her eyes kept moving back to her sister, never wanting to release the vision of her sweet, sleeping face. But Una knew that if she waited any longer, she would surely miss her opportunity for good. She would only have this one time, and then it would be too late.

Una carefully tucked a letter under McKenna's pillow, gently kissed her sister on the forehead, and walked silently out of the door. She stood for a long time outside of the bedroom door and above the stairs that led to her final removal.

Once she crept down the stairs, Una left another note for Catherine.

Dearest Catherine,

Thank you for everything you have done for McKenna and me. I have talked to Saul. He will make sure McKenna and Henry are married, and that she will be taken in to his house as if she were family. Saul knows already that I am leaving. As you might have guessed, I love another man. I will never and can never forget that love or betray it. I would be losing my own soul to do it, and I have nothing left of myself to give.

I don't know where I will go or how I will get there, but I am certain that I will find comfort in the thought of my dearest sister safe and secure in St. Joseph. Please look out for her, if not for my sake, then for my dear mother's sake.

I will never forget your kindness.

Sincerely,

Una Brady

Also, I have borrowed a horse. I will leave her in town where she will be waiting for you. I thank you for this last kindness, though I take it without your knowledge.

Una put the note down securely, picked up what remained of her life, and walked out the door and into the dark.

~

The night was chilly, but Una was happy for it. The chill made her feel alive. It pulled her out of the heartache that continued to drag her into its impenetrable haze. The roads were empty, and the moon only partially lit the earth, so she had to take the trip slowly. If she moved too fast, the horse might trip.

Though up until then the night had sped by, the trip into town felt like it took years. Every moment, Una thought she heard someone else on the road. She was constantly imagining Catherine or McKenna waking in the middle of the night to find one of her notes. She'd not come up with a plan to replace this one.

There was no room for error, and so her mind kept watching errors slip in undiscovered until too late. Her hands were hard to move in the cold. If she exhaled with extra effort, she could see her own breath.

Even the horse seemed to hear and see things that didn't exist in the dark. Una was certain that between her and the horse, they were provoking each other into hearing and seeing things. Una would hear something and turn, and the horse sensed it, slowing down and looking in the same direction. Una thought that as an animal, the horse was probably more keenly aware of what happened in the dark, but over and over again the two would hear or see something with no proof that anything existed beyond their own imaginations.

When Una arrived in town, the sun was not yet up, but Una knew it wouldn't be long. It had taken her too long to get there, and once the sun was up someone might come looking for her. Una didn't think herself brave enough to face anyone if anyone should come, so she had to count on being far away by the time anyone else was on the move, something that seemed less plausible in the cold morning than it had in the warm night.

Una had only the small sack she'd come to America with. She'd left the family Bible under the bed for McKenna to have and cherish. Una wore her green dress. It would remain her most cherished possession until one day the green would lose its color and even Una's memories would fade away.

Una gave the horse a scratch and tied her to one of the hitching posts, close to a patch of grass and small trough of water where she would be easily found later in the day.

Looking around at the dark town, Una noticed the saloon lights on. She supposed that she shouldn't be surprised by that. People spent whole nights in saloons, and it probably went on until the sun came up, maybe even past that.

She took the main road out of town and began walking a few steps forward. It would be a long walk, but she'd thought about making some sort of trade with a wagon along the way. She could do work for a ride, work for food. It was the only way she would be able to get by. On the edge of town, Una turned.

The store where she'd first met Henry was standing dark and innocent on the far side of the square. Una touched her dress and closed her eyes. It had been the same day when she'd looked at the green fabric and knew she'd never have it. But she'd been wrong. She'd not known then what she grew to know later.

Her thoughts kept bringing an overwhelming sense of doubt, of trepidation. She felt as if she couldn't move, that her feet were cemented to the ground. Her desire to stay and her need to go fought for terrain in her mind.

Una forced herself to turn, forced herself to make the next painful, agonizing steps.

She was still only a few steps out of town when she heard a crash. As she swung around, she saw that it came from the saloon. Two men had exploded out of the front doors. There was a cry from a woman inside and a yell from another man.

Una watched wide-eyed, unsure what to do. She stepped to the side of the road, hoping to go unnoticed by the men. There was a scuffle, and one man stood tall, about to hit the other. Una's mouth dropped open as she took in the lumbering frame of Horace Boucher. He swung into the night air, but the hit didn't land. The other man dipped out of the way, turning as he went to make Horace try to turn to catch up to him.

As the other man's face turned into the moonlight toward her, Una saw Henry's beautiful jaw and nose and forehead that she had so deliberately memorized before.

Una stepped forward without realizing it. Her hand released her sack to the ground with a small thump, and Una's heart stopped.

"Henry?" The name came out without her permission, floating on the air, until it made contact with Henry's own ear. His face turned to her just as Horace's hand made contact with Henry's face.

His body swung to the side, and he crumpled to the ground.

"Henry!" Una screamed and began running across the square to him. He was beginning to sit up just as Una flung herself down to him, taking his face in her hands. For one dreadful moment, she'd imagined that he'd died, that Horace's hit had killed him. But Henry's eyes were open, he was breathing, and he was looking at her.

As she studied him, she realized that his face looked almost normal, even though Horace had given him such a solid blow. However, Una knew from having brothers that the swelling was not immediate. It would start soon, and then it would stay for a long time.

"You are a brute!" she yelled as she swung her face up at Horace, who was wobbling back and forth. He flung a hand into the air, turned around, and walked back into the saloon. In another moment Una heard another crash and a loud peal of laughter.

"He's drunk," Henry said, and Una turned back to him.

"I got that. He also just hit you in the face," Una examined his face by the dim light issuing from the saloon. "What were you doing fighting with him anyway? Why are you even here?"

Henry thought about this for a few minutes before answering, "I was fighting with him because he is a sore loser, and I am here because of you." Henry smiled as he let his head rest back into Una's hands.

Una stopped moving. She let her eyes roam over Henry's face trying to determine what he was saying and why. "I don't understand," she finally admitted.

"I didn't expect that you would," Henry braced himself and sat all the way up.

Una waited by as Henry fiddled with his jaw, testing out how tender it was and how bad he thought the damage might be in the coming days. She continued to wait, but Henry did not seem overly eager to quench her curiosity.

"So?" Una persisted. "What do you mean? Explain it to me."

"After dinner last night… I talked to Saul." Henry looked at Una.

"He—" Una didn't believe that Saul had told Henry everything just after she'd asked him to wait. He'd nodded. He'd consented to her request, hadn't he?

"He said you would be upset," Henry smiled. "You have to understand that Saul is very observant. He saw the way you acted when we looked at each other, and he put the pieces together. He's probably known for a long time. He may be quiet, but he isn't stupid. In fact, he's very smart."

"But I—" Una looked back to the place where she'd dropped her sack. "I had a plan. What—"

"Shh," Henry's face didn't lose the smile that kept appearing there in bursts even though it looked like it caused him pain each time.

"Don't tell me to 'shh.' What is the point of all this? Nothing has changed—" Una pulled herself back from Henry, but he reached up, and with a strength she hadn't expected, he pulled her back down to him. Her eyes looked straight into his.

"Everything has changed." Henry reached around to his back pocket and pulled out a wad of bills. "Everything."

Una looked at the money and then at the saloon, "You mean, that is why Horace hit you? Because you," she gestured wildly, "you gambled that from him?"

"Don't feel bad for Horace," Henry said as he shifted.

Una shifted too, "I don't feel bad for Horace, but why would you do that?"

"I talked to Saul for a long time last night. We both agreed that I should go after you."

"Saul agreed too?"

Henry nodded, "That's why he told me in the first place. As kids, we played cards with each other. He was good, but I always won. We played for anything back then, never money, but tonight I decided that I had something worth risking everything for."

"You did?"

"I do," Henry's grip tightened on Una's wrist. "I have you."

Una opened her mouth to speak, but there were no words for him. She wanted to reprimand him for gambling, for doing something so foolish with his money, but here it was. She looked at the wad again.

"How much is this?"

"Everything I've saved over the last eight years, plus what I won tonight. It's enough to buy a farm with." His grin turned into a full smile, and Una laughed. "Horace is a smart gambler but a sore loser. You should know that it was you who really made this happen. He would have been smart if I hadn't outbid him on McKenna's basket. When I came in tonight, he was willing to put down anything, everything, to take my money away. To finally win."

"You bet everything?"

Henry nodded.

"I can't believe I'm saying this, but I almost feel sorry for Horace," Una couldn't stop laughing now. Her smile blossomed out of Henry's, and she felt suddenly like a giddy child. Like the child she'd been before the blight, before she'd lost so much.

Una stopped smiling and looked at her hands.

"What about McKenna?"

Henry lifted Una's face with his fingers, "Don't be silly. I'm going to marry McKenna remember?" He waggled his head, and then tilted it to the other side. "Of course I wouldn't forget McKenna. She will come live with us—as my sister-in-law. She can marry later or never. It doesn't matter to me. She can live with us for the rest of her life if she wants to."

Una felt her eyes fill up. She turned to Henry, and just as she moved forward to kiss him, he stopped her with one hand.

"Remember, you have to be gentle." Henry motioned to his jaw, and Una gasped in horror that she'd so quickly forgotten that he'd just been hit. Slowly she moved forward and just barely let her lips touch his. "Good, but I think we can do a little better than that," Henry smiled at her effort and moved forward, taking Una's head in his hands and pressing her lips to his.

"Una," He pulled away.

She looked up into his eyes and waited for him to speak but he said nothing. "What?" she asked. Her lips craved another taste of him, and she felt herself leaning forward toward his lips once again.

"I love you." Henry kept her from moving forward, made her eyes connect with his. "You must know that I love you. I would never have been able to marry McKenna. I would do anything you asked, anything you wanted, but I could never let you go."

Una nodded her head, understanding what she hadn't understood only hours before. Henry loved her as much as she loved him.

~

The rest of the morning moved fast.

Una and Henry walked into the Donnelly house just as Catherine was reading the letter aloud to McKenna.

Henry gave Una a pinch as he heard her words, "I will never forget that love or betray it," and Una ran to her sister. McKenna hadn't even read the letter that was left under her pillow. She'd woken up thinking that Una had gone out to the fields early as she had so many other mornings before.

As the news spread through the household, there was a great fuss from the children, but oddly Catherine didn't seem as pleased as Una had expected she would. As much as Catherine had talked about getting reimbursed and getting the girls out of the house, it seemed that this was not the way she had meant for it to happen.

Henry went out while Una and McKenna dressed and packed up their few belongings. There seemed no reason to wait and every reason to hurry, so Una and Henry forced themselves on the pastor just as he was finishing his morning repast.

When the pastor ran out of excuses to wait until later in the day, he took the couple into the parish. With the small Donnelly clan, Saul, and McKenna as their witnesses, Henry and Una stood black wool shoulder to creamy green shoulder.

Una looked down at her wedding dress. She didn't mind now if it faded to gray the minute they walked out of the parish. She had something much better than a green dress now.

Chapter Twenty-One

Una's eyes fluttered opened as the first golden rays of light filtered through their bedroom window. She turned under the covers and looked at Henry's face.

"It's morning," she whispered into his ear. His eyes moved behind their lids before opening for the first time that day. The golden flecks sparkled out of his green eyes, and he smiled at the sight of his wife.

"We should get up. There's work to be done." Una said the words, but she didn't yet have the motivation to throw off the covers and leave the warmth of this man for a day of work in the fields – their very own fields.

"We should—yes." Henry leaned forward and took Una's lips with his. His hands moved over her smooth skin under the sheets, and she felt any last vestige of field-related motivation drain out of her.

Una's hands reached for Henry's skin, and she was amazed, as she always was, that she was allowed to touch this skin, this body, and this man as much as she wanted to. Every time felt like a new discovery.

"What a beautiful morning," she said as she smiled at him. Una bit her bottom lip and rolled on top of Henry, letting the sunlight fall over her dewy, morning skin.

~

By the time Una and Henry came downstairs, McKenna had breakfast on the table.

"You didn't have to do this," Una cooed as she kissed her sister good morning.

"I know, but I thought you might be hungry," McKenna smiled mischievously at her sister, who gave McKenna a little swat in response.

"You should go, or you'll be late," Una walked to the door and picked up McKenna's small school satchel. McKenna was behind in school because the blight in Ireland had interrupted her education. However, she was quickly making it up and helping the younger students each time she mastered a new subject.

"I'll be home early to help you cook," McKenna said as she closed the door behind her.

Una walked to the door and opened it again, "Don't leave early, I'll be fine. Just come home at the normal time."

McKenna turned with a smile and a wave, "You need my help. Don't forget the salt pies."

Una had told everyone that she'd put the salt there on purpose, but no seemed to believe her. So Una received a rather bad reputation for making desserts. This led to many jokes at her expense and a truly worried McKenna watching over Una's shoulder in the kitchen.

Una had a sneaking suspicion that McKenna, like herself, felt things were almost too good to be true, that she had to watch very closely or they might change or disappear at any moment. Una found herself keeping a very close eye on things, always ready for the moment when her world might once again come crashing down. But as the days went by, she became secure in her happiness, secure in the love of such a man. She knew that with time, she would worry less and less, and let herself relax into her life, unbelievably wonderful as it was.

Henry seemed to have no trouble believing in his good fortune. He let himself bathe in it every day, and Una loved him for it.

She did understand McKenna's concern over dinner, however. Tonight was to be a special night. Saul was coming to dinner for the first time at the new farm, and everyone wanted the evening to be special. Saul had been the one responsible for so much joy, after all. If he hadn't disobeyed Una's express wishes, she would be alone in the world, with no family, no husband, and nothing left but her memories. Every day, Una thought of that, and every day, Una said a prayer for Saul.

She'd never in her life been so happy that someone had ignored her wishes. Saul had been smarter than them all. He'd seen what she'd failed to see. He'd understood from a better perspective than either she or Henry had had the ability to see, and he'd acted on it.

Later, and to no one's surprise, McKenna did not take Una's advice. She came home early from school despite Una's insistence that she stay. Una could freely admit that, despite the salt switch, McKenna truly was the better cook. She had an instinctive way with ingredients and didn't mind trying new things.

Una knew a million different dishes for a potato, but she was afraid of other foods that she'd never seen before unless there was someone else to guide her through it. McKenna enjoyed cookbooks and had ordered several through a mail order service, which had long since paid for itself.

Since it was a special evening, McKenna had prepared a special dinner of roast turkey and currant jelly, oyster pie, vegetable soup, stewed fruit, and a fancy custard for dessert. The house smelled like heaven, and Una felt like she was in heaven. With her sister standing by her side, her husband's hands gently touching her elbow, delicious food, and a farm that blossomed with a bountiful harvest, she wasn't sure how life had ever gotten so good.

"I hear wheels," Henry said as he walked across the room. Una turned toward the front of the house, her ears perking up. She was rather amazed at Henry's hearing. Una had suspected that it came from all those years of tuning in to pick up Saul's quiet words.

McKenna quickly took off her apron, and Una did the same. Henry led the way, and they all walked out of the house to the porch to greet Saul. Una put a hand up to her brow as she looked into the setting sun. It was hard to see clearly, but she could hear the carriage come in front of her and see the outline of it. Then she noticed two outlines on top of the carriage. Una took a step back and watched as Cecily Baker hopped down from the carriage next to Saul.

"Cecily," Henry let out a loud exclamation, and Una laughed before moving to embrace the other woman. They had long since become friendly, though with a new farm and a new marriage, Una hadn't made much time for friendships. This was something she hoped to work on in the years to come.

"Come in," Una opened the door for Cecily, who was being released from an embrace with McKenna. The group talked affectionately over dinner, and for the second time, Una noticed the strange way Saul spoke when around Cecily. It was not so much strange as it was normal. He spoke rather naturally, loud enough to hear even with the din of other people talking. Una hadn't had the presence of mind to really watch the first time she'd seen it but observing it at the dinner table let Una glimpse a spark she'd never really considered before.

"I'll get dessert," Una stood.

Abruptly McKenna stood up next to her, "I'll help."

Una gave her sister a questioning look.

"I worked really hard on that custard." McKenna walked around Una without apology, and Una laughed.

"I'd better help too, or I'll feel like the incompetent woman," Cecily followed just behind.

When they all three sat back down, Una held up her hands and took a breath that silenced everyone.

"I just want to say—how thankful I am for all of you." Una spoke and looked at each person around her table. "I love each of you so much." Her heart felt overwhelmed with love for them. "I wake up each morning in disbelief at my wonderful life." Una smiled widely with a soft tear in her eye, and she watched smiles spread across her favorite faces.

"On that note," Cecily leaned forward. "There *is* something we wanted to tell you tonight."

Una listened to the "we" with interest and looked to Henry who had an expression of anticipated happiness on his face.

"Henry knows that I…" Cecily caught her breath and began again, "…I have loved Saul since I was a child. I haven't just loved him I guess… I've been in love with him. When I was a little girl, I saw him rescue a doe that had gotten caught in brambles and was unable to get out. He was so big, and the doe was so small. Another child would have… I don't know, but Saul, he was…well, he made me love him. At that moment, I decided that I wanted him to be my husband. Unfortunately, I forgot to tell Saul." Everyone laughed and watched mesmerized by the connection these two people now shared.

"Thankfully, Saul has a little brother who is willing to divulge a friend's deepest secret."

Henry gave a little bow, "I was just following his gracious example. Saul guided us, and I owed it to him to do the same." Henry looked at his brother and smiled. "I was only returning the favor."

"And you have," Saul smiled sheepishly. "We're getting married. Not as fast as you two did but in a month."

Una clapped her hands together once and looked on in disbelief. It seemed quite possible that anything wonderful could happen at any moment.

"You will both live on the farm?" Una asked, realizing how it might sound silly. She was aware that Cecily's family was rather wealthy and that they might choose a different life altogether.

"Yes," Cecily said. "But, we may... my father has begun to build on this idea. It wouldn't happen for a good number of years yet, but he and some of his colleagues want to build a connection of relay stations that go all the way across the country."

"Across the great plains, the Rocky Mountains, all the way out to California," Saul's voice was practically animated. Una listened enraptured.

"It would be a mail delivery service. Something to get news and post from one side of the country to the other. It would start right here in St. Jo." Cecily finished.

"That's amazing," McKenna said. Una could see clearly in her sister's face that she was imagining it all in her mind. Since starting school here, McKenna had been spouting off facts about the geography of the land. Una sensed in her sister a burgeoning desire to travel it, to know it more intimately. "What would it be called?"

"Nobody knows yet, maybe The Relay System or the Atlantic to Pacific."

"What about Horseman Express? Horse Rider Trail? Pony Trail?" McKenna began pitching names forward randomly, and Una laughed at her sister's enthusiasm.

"Those aren't half bad," Cecily said. "Maybe one day you would like to come to a meeting? My father said they could use another good mind."

McKenna looked to Una, who smiled at her sister, "I would love that more than anything."

Una felt Henry take her hand, and she turned her head to look into her husband's eyes. He had become so easy to read. Maybe because his face and eyes were obvious, or maybe because she felt the same way.

McKenna followed Cecily and Saul all the way out to their carriage, talking about the new express mail system with an enthusiasm Una had never witnessed in her sister before.

"A successful dinner," Una said looking around.

"One without salt in the dessert is always successful in my book," Henry teased.

Una turned to her husband with both hands on her hips, "I did that on purpose."

"Because you wanted me to spend thirty dollars on something inedible." Henry made a face.

Una laughed at her husband, who picked her up in one sweeping motion.

"You know what would make tonight perfect?" Henry held Una lightly in his arms, and she leaned in to smell him.

"What is that?" Her breath was close to his ear, and she felt him shiver as it tickled him.

Henry leaned his head back and looked at her, "A second dessert."

Una leaned forward again and nipped Henry's neck with her teeth, and then looked in his eyes with a broad smile across her face.

"I think that can be arranged."

A Note to my Readers

I really appreciate you taking the time to read my book and I would like to thank you from the bottom of my heart. If you enjoyed the story, please leave a review where you purchased the book. You'll be helping others make a decision on their purchase and I appreciate your effort, so will other forthcoming readers. If you would like to be the first to know about my new releases, promotions and giveaways, please sign up for my mailing list here http://katstclair.com/signup-mailing-list/. If you have any comments or questions about my books, please do not hesitate to contact me at katherinesaintclair@gmail.com.

Katherine St. Clair

An Excerpt from Under a Texas Sky

Chapter One

"Not that one." Evangeline pointed to the trunk she wanted moved first. The men, in their dirty, ragged clothing, set the trunk down. "I want this one taken first. You can come back for this one next."

The volume of her command triggered something in her lungs. Evangeline bent over as she coughed into the floor. Her stomach muscles had been sore for days from the coughing. Talking often triggered the response, so silence was in order, not her usual state of stasis.

She was a tall, thick-boned woman. Some called her imposing. She liked the word. She enjoyed the thought of having a noticeable presence. She handed two hatboxes and a small valise to a third person, too young to be called a man. She sighed as she watched him fumble with her items.

"Be careful with those," she snapped. She stood very still as she tried to fill her lungs steadily. She had a vision of her most beloved items falling into the ocean as this boy wobbled his way down the gangplank.

Evangeline made sure her hat was fastened tightly to her head. As she regarded herself in the mirror, she noticed her face was looking a strange color of grey. She needed to get off this cursed ship, she thought. The sickness had overtaken her around day four of the eight-day voyage from Liverpool to Boston. She took a steady, deep breath, then made her way above board.

"There you are," Mrs. Warren gave a facial expression meant to be a smile. Mrs. Warren was a friend of the Allum family and had agreed to make the voyage across the Atlantic with young Evangeline Allum. Mrs. Warren's sister lived a few hours outside of Boston, and she'd planned the visit for the purpose of delivering Evangeline into Mr. Holmström's care.

Mr. Luden Holmström was meant to be on the dock looking for her just about now. She looked over the side of the ship, but the only thing she saw was a mass of indecipherable faces.

"And how are you feeling today?" Mrs. Warren grimaced, her large jowls curving downward. The sight of the older woman's face did not, in fact, make Evangeline feel any better.

"Terrible," Evangeline said. She cast some of this blame on Mrs. Warren, who had been nothing but tiresome and ugly the entire trip. Evangeline coughed into her French lace handkerchief. Her lungs were raw and her head felt tight.

Mrs. Warren turned away, as repulsed by Evangeline's coughing as Evangeline was by Mrs. Warren's face.

An American husband. The thought once again flowed through Evangeline's mind. There had been an American man who dined at their table on board, and Evangeline hadn't been impressed. Flat, harsh speech, combined with the coarse manners of someone who made their money in trade. Her family needed new money, and Raymond Humes would ensure her family enough money to keep her family's estate intact. He, seemingly, wanted the prestige and association an old English family could lend to his name.

"I can see my sister from here," Mrs. Warren said. Her face came the closest to a happy expression – or at least not tortured – that Evangeline had ever seen it. Evangeline followed the older woman's eyes and found herself looking at a strange mirror image of the woman next to her.

"We won't leave you here, of course," Mrs. Warren said. The way she said it made Evangeline feel that leaving her was exactly what Mrs. Warren intended to do.

"Please, I won't hear of it. I thank you for all of your attentions. I will be sure to write my father and mother to let them know how extremely helpful you've been," She pushed the French lace to her mouth as a wave of sour air hit her nostrils making her stomach turn.

Mrs. Warren blushed.

When the wave passed Evangeline tried to recover a smile. "But you must go to your sister now. I am quite capable, and Mr. Holmström is probably looking for me as we speak."

Mrs. Warren opened her mouth to give a false protest.
"No, no," Evangeline cut her off. "I insist."

More books from Katherine St.Clair

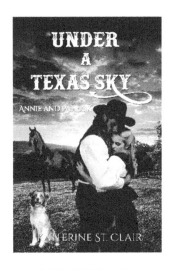

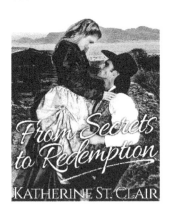

Made in the USA
Monee, IL
16 October 2022